GENIE

Unlucky Charm

ose Wilkins had an idyllic childhood in the Welsh
untryside before being sent to an all-girls' board-
g school. She survived the experience and started
ting while studying Classics at university, as an
ape from all the gloom and gore on her reading
. She now lives and works in London.

S

Unlucky Charm

Rose Wilkins

First published 2008 by Macmillan Children's Books
a division of Macmillan Publishers Limited
20 New Wharf Road, London N1 9RR
Basingstoke and Oxford
www.panmacmillan.com

Associated companies throughout the world

ISBN 978-0-330-43881-0

A CIP catalogue record for this book is available from
the British Library.

Typeset by Intype Libra Ltd
Printed and bound in Great Britain by Mackays of Chatham plc, Kent

For my grandmother, Virginia Merrill –
far away, but close at heart

'But of course your parents will love me!' Prince Ashazrahim the Resplendent, Jewel of Arabia and Lion of Baghdad, was assuring his girlfriend, Fran Roper of Number 35 Milson Road. 'I'm a handsome and well-bred aristocrat. What's not to like?'

Introducing your new – and first ever – boyfriend to your parents is always nerve-wracking. It gets a lot worse when that boyfriend happens to be an ancient mythical being who first materialized from a magic ring. During his career as a genie, Ash had spent hundreds of years granting wishes to lovelorn damsels, and as far as he was concerned, this qualified him as a model of masculine sensitivity and all-conquering charm. Fran knew about the charm and sensitivity. She just wasn't convinced that it was immediately obvious to the wider world.

Ash, of course, had very little experience of the wider world. In fact, it had been strictly off-limits until about six weeks ago, when a well-timed snog broke the spell that kept him the Slave of the Ring. Since it was Fran's kiss that had restored Ash to human form, he decided that it was necessary to kiss her as often as possible, just to make sure.

* * * * * ✦ 1 ✦ * * * * *

Insurance, he called it. And Fran certainly wasn't complaining.

Now the two of them were standing outside Number 35 Milson Road on a dull wintry afternoon. Fran was chewing a strand of her long fair hair, grey eyes clouded with anxiety. Ash was admiring the glitter of his diamond ear-drop in a car window. The Lion of Baghdad was about to be formally introduced to the House of Roper.

'. . . so that's when I realized that, as extreme sports go, crocodile hunting was not for me,' Ash concluded.

'Coo-el,' said Fran's little brother Mickey, saucer-eyed.

'My goodness,' said Mrs Roper.

'Hmm,' said her husband.

Fran smiled nervously and poured everyone another cup of tea. So far Ash had held forth on the perfect recipe for iced-sherbet and champagne cocktails, drawn parallels between the latest crisis in the Middle East and tribal blood feuds in ancient Mesopotamia, and made passing reference to his travels to everywhere from Idaho to Azerbaijan. (It was perhaps unfortunate that a lot of these anecdotes began with 'A girl I met in . . .' Fran could hardly explain that Ash was referring to former Commanders of the Ring, rather than a global network of ex-girlfriends.)

In their different ways, everyone was trying hard. Mickey was hovering with milk and sugar like a pint-sized maître d', Mr Roper had given the lounge its first de-clutter in months and Mrs Roper was wearing a pretty blouse rather than her usual weekend uniform of ancient T-shirt and tracksuit bottoms. Her effort was, however, utterly eclipsed by Ash's shirt: a vision of peacock-blue silk embroidered with gold thread around the hem. The air around him was delicately scented with sandalwood and spices, and the diamond ear-drop flashed as he moved. Beth, Fran's two-year-old sister, had spent much of the past hour trying to grab it.

In fact, Beth had taken such a shine to their guest that she threw a tantrum when he prepared to leave. Everyone was very impressed by the graceful way in which Ash kissed Mrs Roper's hand in farewell – you would hardly have known he had a wailing toddler wrapped around one leg. As for Mrs Roper, she turned the same shade of pink her elder daughter did in moments of pleasure or panic.

'So how did I do?' Ash asked as Fran showed him to the door.

'Um, great.'

'Truly?' His handsome face was looking at her anxiously and Fran suppressed a smile. Underneath his Lion of Baghdad posturing, Ash was a bit of a pussycat.

'Of course. Everybody loved you,' she said with all the conviction she could muster.

'That's a relief. Especially as back home I'd be having to brush up my dowry negotiation skills by now.' He grinned. 'The thing is . . . I didn't want to let on earlier, but I *was* a little nervous. I know this afternoon means a lot to you.' And seeing his dark eyes turned soft and shining just for her, Fran couldn't help but smile back.

'Do you ever miss your old life, back home in Baghdad?' she asked.

'Nah. Life as a playboy prince isn't all it's cracked up to be.'

'I can imagine. All those boring palaces and tedious people bowing down to you the whole time . . .'

'OK, so there were perks. And yes, I kind of miss my thoroughbred racing camel and personal pastry cook. But when I think of how I used to act, how I used to treat people . . . Ugh. Let's just say I'm glad you didn't know me then.'

'So you reckon you're a reformed character?'

'Not *entirely*, I'm happy to say,' he said, making a lunge for her waist, so that she shrieked and squirmed. Then his expression turned serious again. 'I've been all over the world and all through history during my time as a Slave of the Ring, but here and now comes top of my list. And that's because of you.'

Fran blushed. 'Good to see you haven't lost your talent for shameless flattery.'

'Flattery's got nothing to do with it. The thing is,' Ash said, half-teasing, half-serious, 'I may not be your genie any more, but your wish is still my command. That's a promise.'

After a lingering goodbye, Fran went to rejoin her family in the lounge. They were all looking slightly stunned. 'My goodness,' said Mrs Roper again.

'Coo-el,' chorused Mickey and Beth.

'*Where* did he say he was from?' asked Mr Roper.

'Baghdad. I've told you that before.'

* * * * * ✦ 4 ★ * * * * *

'So he's an Iraqi?'

'Erm, sort of. But he hasn't been there for years.' Make that centuries . . . Fran set about clearing the tea things to hide her awkwardness.

'And his family are back in the Middle East?' continued Mr Roper.

'Not exactly. He was brought up by an uncle after his parents died. I'm, um, not sure he's kept much contact with that part of the world.'

'So what exactly is he doing in London? He said he was on "a break", but he's not a student, is he?'

Fran reddened. 'What are you trying to say? I don't get it – it's almost like you want to accuse Ash of something.'

'Now then, love, there's no need to get upset,' soothed her mother. 'Nobody's accusing anybody of anything. We both liked Ash very much. It's just that we spent nearly two hours with the boy and yet we don't feel that we know that much about him. I can see that he's intelligent and charming, and terribly good-looking of course, but . . .'

Mr Roper cleared his throat. 'He's a bit older than you, for starters.'

'Oh, but he's really very immature for his age,' Fran reassured them.

Her parents exchanged glances. 'Yes, well, he certainly has some very, er, colourful stories,' said her father.

'After all his adventures I'm not surprised he wants to take a break,' added Mrs Roper brightly.

'But a break from *what*, that's what I want to know. I mean, he's clearly not strapped for cash—'

'I don't have to deal with this,' said Fran hotly.

★ ★ ★ ★ ★ 5 ★ ★ ★ ★ ★

'You're being totally paranoid and small-minded and I'm not going to listen any more.' Then she turned on her heel, swept upstairs to her bedroom and shut the door with a bang.

Strops and slammed doors had never been Fran's style, and it wasn't long before she was feeling guilty for flouncing out of the lounge like that. She realized Ash could be a bit . . . full on, and she knew her mum and dad were just doing their concerned-parent thing. But couldn't they even have pretended to be pleased for her?

The ringing of her mobile was a welcome distraction. It was Amira, the manager of the Stamping Butterflies, a girl band Fran sang in. Amira was a fifteen-year-old, five-foot-nothing female version of Simon Cowell, but Fran knew that within that scary exterior beat a heart of (double) platinum.

'Oh, Amira,' she moaned, 'it was just so unfair. Ash tried really hard! I know he comes from a different . . . background to most of the people round here, but I thought my parents would be more, you know, *welcoming*. Not all tight-lipped and accusatory.'

'Look, you know I like Ash. But let's face it, he's also quite weird,' said Amira cheerfully.

'You think Ash is weird?'

'Sure. A very nice, seriously hot weirdo. Then there's the fact he's also a) older b) flashy and c) mysterious. Of course your olds are freaking out. If he was just some pimply schoolkid they'd know what they were dealing with.'

'I s'pose.'

'No supposing about it. They'll get over it and so will you.'

After Fran said goodbye to Amira, she spent a while looking at the ring she still wore for old times' sake, despite the fact it was undeniably cheap-looking, with a plasticky purple gemstone that might have come from a cracker. The instructions that had come with it had been mysterious yet straightforward: *Employ Suitably for Hart Desiring*. But winning your heart's desire was only the half of it, thought Fran with a sigh.

Monday morning in the Roper household was the usual melee of lost keys, burnt toast and the happy shrieks of Beth throwing Coco Pops at her mother. Fran, busy scrubbing glooped marmalade from her shirt, was not best pleased to find Mickey tugging her towards the window. 'But, Fran,' he said insistently, 'I think it's for you.'

'What –?'

A silver Lotus had roared up outside and was parked alongside the house at a rakish angle. Thrash metal blared from the sound system. Ash was leaning out of the driving seat, a happy smile on his lips, his hand on the horn. It had a honk to rattle the windowpanes.

Fran tumbled out of the door.

'Where – what – how –' she began, then ground to a disbelieving halt.

'Isn't it fabulous?' said Ash with pride. 'Have a seat.'

Fran scrambled in, acutely aware of a rash of twitching curtains along the street. The rest of the

Roper family had temporarily abandoned keys, toast and cereal-chucking to crowd on the doorstep. Even the postman was openly staring.

'You know, I usually just walk to school . . .' she muttered.

'Where's the fun in that? This is an absolute dream of a ride – and the acceleration's so much smoother than on a flying carpet!'

Ash had accessorized with wraparound shades, in spite of a total absence of sun, and was handling the gear changes as if he'd done it all his life.

'You never told me you could drive! And where did you *get* this, Ash? Did someone lend it to you?'

'Oh, you know,' he said airily. 'My contacts in the ex-genie underworld are very far-reaching.'

She shot him a suspicious glance. This was the kind of non-answer he always gave when she enquired about the source of the rent on his flat, his endless parade of clothes, or the mobile fast filling up with the numbers of new friends and acquaintances. Over the last few weeks, Fran had been too caught up in the thrill of First Romance to fret about the practicalities of Ash's new life, especially as he seemed to be adjusting to twenty-first-century humanhood with almost indecent ease. OK, so maybe her parents had a point – what *did* Ash do all day when she was at school?

But before she had the chance to quiz him further they had roared up to the school gates, where a cluster of gawping students had already formed. Fran wanted to be out of the car and away from the spotlight as soon as possible, but Ash was magnificently oblivious to their audience as he leaned over for a farewell kiss. 'Here,' he said, opening the glove compartment and presenting her with a pink-ribboned box. 'I nearly forgot – something to sweeten the school day.'

It was a huge tray of Turkish delight. Fran sighed and smiled. Her interrogation would just have to wait.

From the window of 10B's form room, Zara Truman was watching in disbelief as Fran Roper clambered out of a brand-new sports car, before being pulled back for a passionate embrace with its driver.

'Drug dealer,' she said, 'or slave trader. He's got to be. There's no other possible explanation.'

'Beth Hicks reckons he's a Bollywood film star on location in London. And Jessica heard he's the son of a Saudi oil billionaire,' Sadie Smith proclaimed, tossing her blonde ponytail and dimpling. 'But it's *way* romantic, don't you think? Like that fairy tale. You know – the weird chicken.'

'Ugly duckling.'

'Whatever. Not that Fran was ever, like, *minging*, just a bit mousy, but it's still totally heart-warming . . .'

Zara gave an incredulous snort. As a professional cutie-pie, Sadie set out to treat life as one big cheer-leading audition and until lately her super-sweet insincerity was the perfect foil for Zara's brand of snarls 'n' sadism. In fact, the power-base of their friendship was a good cop/bad cop routine designed to keep everyone else in their place: Zara would stick the knife in, which Sadie would then twist with an adorable smile. Since hooking up with Rob Crawford, however, it was beginning to look as if Sadie's sugar-coated fangs had lost their bite.

'In fact, it reminds me how Robbie and—'

But Zara did not want to hear about Robbie. Rob and his new band, the Oxymorons, was all Sadie talked about lately. Unfortunately, the only people who genuinely believed the band's name was ironic were the Morons themselves.

It had all been so different a month or so ago. Zara thought back to the good old days, when the Oxymorons had been called Firedog and had actually had some street cred. She and Sadie's pal Francesca had been on vocals, while Quinn had been the band's lead singer-songwriter, and sex god of the upper school. And for a brief, sweet time, Zara and Sadie had reigned supreme in his entourage, their place in the Conville Secondary School A-list assured for evermore.

All good things come to an end, but this ending had been a particularly acrimonious one. Almost immediately after their first official gig, Firedog had split up when Amira – Quinn's ex – had burst on to the scene, accusing him of ripping off her music and threatening everything from legal action to GBH. Quinn had taken it very hard, shaved off his tousled blond locks and done a lot of moping in corners.

Meanwhile, Francesca had changed schools, Sadie had morphed into an honorary Moron, and Fran – who used to tag along after Quinn like a drooling poodle – was now shacked up with the Bollywood Oil Baron . . . leaving Zara feeling just a teensy bit out of things.

'Sadie,' she said, abruptly cutting into the Moron

monologue, 'remember that house-party of Francesca's? After the Firedog gig?'

'Omigod it was *awesome*. With the belly dancers and those yummy canapé things with dates . . .'

'Yeah, such an awesome party that Francesca's parents had a fit and packed her off to boarding school, Firedog split up and I got bitten by a rabid camel.' As a matter of fact, Zara rather liked her camel-bite scar – it worked well when accessorized by her multiple piercings, lashings of black eyeliner and permanent sneer. But that was beside the point. 'Anyhow, I reckon Fran was out to sabotage the whole thing, right from the start.'

Sadie wrinkled her pert little nose. 'Why'd she want to do that?'

'C'mon, Sade! You know how Quinn used to string her along just to get to Francesca.'

'Oh, yeah.' Sadie giggled. 'He always was such a flirt. Poor old Fran didn't stand a chance.'

'Well, I reckon Fran used that party as payback time. First she gets her mate – Amina or Meera or whoever – to attack Quinn with all those crazy accusations. Then she uses Ali Baba and his gang to trash Francesca's house. He was the one who brought in the dancing bimbos and deranged animals and guys with turbans, remember.'

'I kinda thought it was the rugby boys who did most of the trashing.'

'But—'

Sadie's attention was already moving on. 'After all, Quinn *did* steal that other girl's songs and it is so not cool to go ripping off other people's, like, creative spirit. Robbie, now, is a *naturally* talented

* * * * * ★ 11 ★ * * * * *

songwriter, but Quinn never let him fulfil his potential. I reckon it was cos Quinn felt, you know, *threatened* . . . anyway, Robbie's latest song is called 'Puke-fest Lullaby' and it's majorly poetic. Robbie says he's going to make me his museum.'

'Muse.'

'Whatever. The point, Zara, is that me and Robbie are in love. Just like Ash and Fran. That's why they've got this, like, adorable glow around them.'

'Adorable glow? More like scent of desperation. I'm telling you, Sade, there's something dodgy about those two. I *know* it.'

'And I'm telling you,' Sadie replied with a gut-churning simper, 'that you'd be so more chilled about the conspiracy-theory stuff if you could find yourself a boyfriend.'

Fran found it hard to concentrate during the after-school music session at Amira's house. She still hadn't got over how lucky she was to be a member of what was (unofficially) the Hottest Girl Band in Greater London, and since the other Butterflies went to a different school from her, time spent hanging out with them was always special. But right now her mind was on other things. She and Ash had planned to go to the cinema later that evening, but then at lunchtime he'd rung her mobile and cancelled, muttering about some business that he had to attend to. He'd been grovellingly apologetic (well, as grovelling as an Arabian aristocrat could be), and promised to make it up to her, but when she asked about the nature of this 'urgent business' he suddenly claimed not to be able to hear her properly – 'Sorry, princess, the reception's really bad here . . . gotta go. Chat later, OK?' Something was definitely up.

'FRAN!'

Fran jumped. She had been miles away, and completely oblivious to the fact that Amira had been glowering at her for the past three minutes. As well as being the Stamping Butterflies' manager, Amira was their songwriter and self-appointed slave-driver. At the moment she had her hands on her hips, one foot tapping the floor in a menacing sort of way.

'Sorry . . . did I miss something?'

Amira gave an exasperated sigh. 'Only the entire debrief. But seeing as I'm such a softie, I'll treat you to the abridged version: Naz keeps coming in a beat late in the "Angel Cake" descant; Zoë was off-key for the chorus of "Quintessential"; you, Ms Roper, were away with the fairies for all of everything, and Parminder's "Looking Glass Boy" solo sounded like someone dragging their nails down a blackboard.'

'But I'b god a cold!' snuffed Parminder plaintively. ''Snot by fault I can't keep id tude!'

Amira's response was to chuck a packet of throat sweets at her head. Hard.

Fran decided to make an intervention. 'Hey, did you guys see the Sugar Dolls on *Hype!* last Sunday?'

Her manager didn't look fooled by this blatant attempt to distract her from their performance appraisal. Still, as Fran knew, Amira found it hard to resist the chance to analyse the latest developments in the music scene. *Hype!* was a Sunday afternoon chat show, hosted by uber-hip presenters Posy

Parkin and Zed Boulder, and essential viewing for anyone interested in hot new bands, star interviews and celeb gossip. Amira saw this as professional research for her future conquest of the record industry.

'Bit of a let-down, I thought. Releasing a "Greatest Hits" album is the beginning of the end,' she said dismissively. 'They're already starting to sound like a bunch of has-beens.'

'I was too busy drooling over Zed to pay attention to the guests,' Zoë sighed.

'Aw, c'mon, he's just there to look cute and read off the autocue,' said Naz. 'Everyone knows Posy is the real star of the show. What a goddess!'

'Maybe one day she'll be interviewing the Butterflies. A whole *Hype!* special dedicated to us and our collection of Quicksilver Music Awards,' Fran joked.

'Not with our vocals the state they're in,' Amira retorted. 'At the moment, we haven't even a hope of getting into the studio audience. Last time I tried that ticket-hotline of theirs, I wasted two hours on speed dial.'

Fran decided to keep quiet about the fact that Sadie Smith and Rob Crawford had spent most of the last two weeks trumpeting the fact that they'd be at the filming of *Hype!* next weekend. Even though Amira didn't know them personally, Rob, an ex-Firedog and ex-sidekick of Quinn's, was high on her grudge list. Amira was a great manager and an even better friend, but forgiving 'n' forgetting wasn't her strong point.

*

'I know I deserve to suffer.'

Fran smiled tightly, and sneaked a peek at her watch.

'I mean, I screwed up. Big time.'

Fran looked at her watch again, and shifted her school bag on to the other arm.

'I was a user and a cheat, and I hurt a lot of people along the way. I'm not proud of that.' Quinn's voice throbbed with feeling. 'But when I stood on a stage, when I felt the music in my blood, the passion was genuine. It was *real*. You remember, don't you, Fran?'

Fran sighed. 'You certainly had plenty of . . . stage presence.'

Quinn didn't respond directly, just looked tragic. Thanks to his jutting cheekbones, designer stubble and brooding brown eyes, this was something he did rather effectively. Some might say that tragic was too good for him – after all, this was the guy who had exploited his bogus rock god credentials to break pretty much every heart that crossed his path. Including Fran's. It had taken a lot of anguish (and genie magic) for her to realize the only reason Quinn condescended to flirt with her was because of her friendship with the much more glamorous Francesca.

Still, Fran was kind of surprised by how far he was taking the Fallen Idol act. After the Firedog break-up, he'd even cropped short his famous dirty-blond locks in a gesture of atonement and/or mourning.

As Quinn rambled on about the Burden of Celebrity and the Dark Side of Fame, Fran did her best to smile and nod, all the while wondering where on earth Ash had got to – he was supposed to have picked her up twenty minutes ago. It was Friday, and thanks to teacher-training, their school had a half-holiday, and Fran had re-arranged her and Ash's cancelled cinema trip for that afternoon.

'Have . . . have you heard anything from Francesca?' Quinn was asking.

'Um, I had an email a week or so ago. She's really enjoying Ashton Court, says she's met some fantastic people.'

Quinn gave a floating-up-from-a-crypt sigh. Fran thought it was a bit much really: he and Francesca had only been going out for all of five minutes. She was about to make this point – albeit more tactfully – when finally her mobile rang.

'Ash! I hope you're on your way.'

'Light of my Eyes, Delight of my Heart—'

Fran frowned. '*Please* don't tell me you're bailing out. Again.'

'When you fail your friends, the only person you let down is yourself,' Quinn observed mournfully.

'Who was that?'

'Just Quinn.'

'The dung-beetle blond? What's *he* doing with you?'

'Nothing. We bumped into each other – oh, never mind.' Fran got up and walked out of earshot. 'Look, are we still on for the film or not?'

'Er, well, the truth is, O Best Beloved, something's come up . . . business . . . you know how it is.'

'No, I don't. That's the *point*.'

'It's all a bit complicated—'

'So explain it! Come on, Ash, don't you think I deserve to know what's going on with your life? What's the big mystery – and is it something I should be worried about?'

There was a long silence at the other end of the phone. Fran found she was clenching her free hand so tightly the nails had dug into her palm. 'You're right,' said Ash at last. 'I'm sorry. I was waiting for the right time to explain but . . . Look, can you come and meet me in, say, three quarters of an hour?' He gave her a central London address. 'I guarantee to explain everything. Just . . . promise you won't be mad, OK?'

'Well, it's not like I can send you back to your ring in disgrace any more,' Fran said lightly. However, she couldn't help feeling a little nervous.

Unbeknown to Fran, she wasn't the only person busy speculating about what Ash got up to when he wasn't wooing his girlfriend with Turkish delight.

Zara was still seething at Sadie's remark about finding herself a boyfriend – the last person who'd cast aspersions on Zara's pulling power had had their hair stapled to a cubicle in the boys' toilets. Right now, Zara was tempted to apply the same remedy to Sadie's pert little nose. And the fact that *Fran Roper* of all people – bland, boring, butter-wouldn't-melt Fran – had joined Sadie in the loved-up brigade was adding insult to injury.

In truth, Zara didn't really believe her Fran-the-criminal-mastermind theory. Fran didn't have the guts – or brains – to stage-manage a decent vengeance. But there was no way Zara was buying into Sadie's vision of Mr and Mrs Adorable Glow of True Love either. OK, so Fran's boyfriend was hot, if you could get over the girlie silk shirts and exotic aftershave. But there was definitely something weird about him, and something even weirder in the way Fran got all pink and twitchy whenever anyone asked her how they'd met or what he did. Personally, Zara wasn't that bothered if Fran was about to be kidnapped and sold into a Middle Eastern harem, or used as a drugs mule, or brainwashed into some creepy cult. But if romantic delusions were going to be shattered, Zara was the gal to do it. That way, she could serve Fran right and prove Sadie wrong in one fell swoop.

So when she walked out of a newsagent's only to see Ashazrah-whatsit talking on a mobile phone, it seemed like fate. Especially since the bits and pieces she could hear of his conversation were most intriguing: 'Expecting a consignment . . . top-quality gear . . . special delivery, yeah . . . any time now . . .'

After ending the call, he paused in the middle of the street, chewing his lip, and looking troubled. Zara followed him into the tube station opposite and on to a train, taking care to keep a reasonable distance between them. Once they had left the Underground, she was not disheartened to find herself in Knightsbridge; the guy clearly wasn't lacking in pretensions to grandeur, and there was bound to be lots of money in people-smuggling or drug-running or whatever he did.

Their final destination was one of the elegant

little back streets off Sloane Square, the kind where even the exhaust fumes reek of money. Was he going to meet Fran at some kind of private members club? His preoccupied expression, however, was not the look of a man on his way to a hot date. The next thing she knew, Ash had arrived at the entrance to an exclusive-looking boutique, where he took out a pair of keys and glanced around him in a furtive manner. Zara waited until her quarry had slipped through the door before positioning herself behind a van parked opposite. Something was about to happen, she could feel it in her bones.

The sign across the door read 'Oronames Enterprise Ltd: Arabic Art & Antiquities' in a gold script, and there was nothing in the window except for a very beautiful blue ceramic dish, spotlit on a velvet stand. No opening hours were advertised, a security camera winked above the door, and you had to press a bell to gain admittance. Fran's stomach squirmed nervously as she did so.

'Welcome to my humble emporium,' said Ash, opening the door, then sweeping her a graceful bow.

She stared back at him in disbelief. 'You're working in a *shop*?' Lots of outlandish possibilities had flitted through her mind on the way here, but this hadn't been one of them.

'Oronames prefers to think of it as an art gallery. What do you think?'

Fran began to take in her surroundings. The room they were in was large, softly lit and smelt faintly of incense. Rich oriental tapestries hung from the walls, and everywhere she looked treasures glowed discreetly in glass cases. An emerald glass bottle . . . an ornamental bronze lamp . . . silver platters . . . ivory chess pieces . . . No prices were on display, but each item had a little information card, like in a museum.

'It's amazing. But I don't understand. I mean – *Oronames*? That was the name of the corner shop where I got the ring. Is it just some kind of mad coincidence or—'

'Oh, there's only one Oronames. It turns out the corner shops are just one aspect of a highly lucrative retail empire.'

'But – how—'

Ash looked smug. 'From what you'd told me about buying the ring, I suspected the vendor's pedigree was an interesting one. I took the first opportunity of following up the lead and found that Oronames is, indeed, the name of a man of many talents. He's been most helpful in getting me set up – apparently I have a flare for front-of-shop management.'

It wasn't hard to see that Ash's flowery compliments would go down a treat with the well-heeled ladies of Knightsbridge, and Fran supposed genuine oil tycoons weren't averse to a bit of aristocratic flattery either. She beamed at him. 'But, Ash, this is brilliant! Why on earth didn't you tell me before? I was worried something . . . well, I was beginning to worry, that's all. But this is great!'

Of course she still had lots of questions, but for now she was just relieved to know what was going on. She wouldn't have to keep fobbing off her parents, she could finally come clean to the people at school! 'Oh, my boyfriend works in an art gallery,' she imagined saying. 'We met over an antique Syrian vase. Didn't I mention it before?'

'So what's the urgent business you have to stay here for? Are you waiting for a customer?'

Ash began to fiddle with his watch. 'Not exactly. We're expecting a consignment of decorative tiles. Oronames is, er, overseeing the delivery.' Now he was looking positively shifty. 'In fact, it's about time I went round the back for the, um . . . landing . . .'

'Landing? Doesn't the stuff arrive in an armoured van or something?'

'Carpet, actually.'

Fran opened her mouth but no words came, only spluttering. Before she had a chance to recover, Ash rushed to explain. It transpired that Oronames was in possession of a flying carpet (premium class) whose homing device was set to ancient Baghdad. All their stock was bought up cheap in the bazaar – usually in exchange for twenty-first-century novelties such as cigarette lighters and chocolate spread – loaded up on the carpet, then flown back to modern London where it was given a bit of pro-ageing treatment, whisked into a glass case and sold on for a princely sum.

'But that's forgery!' Fran exclaimed.

'This is why I didn't explain things earlier. I *knew* you were going to go all moral on me.'

'Too right. You're nothing but a couple of con-artists.'

'Certainly not.' Ash had recovered himself and was looking haughty. 'I am an entrepreneur and a gentleman. Everything in this gallery is the *genuine* article. Which is more than can be said for the cruddy knock-offs you find in most of the dealerships in town . . . Look, I've got to go and help with the unloading – are you coming or not?'

Ethical misgivings aside, Fran had always wanted to see a flying carpet. So she unpursed her lips and followed Ash to the back of the shop, where he pulled back a wall-hanging to reveal a door. He was careful to lock it behind them, but it was perhaps unfortunate that neither of them had noticed the main door to the shop was still open.

The back office was small, windowless and completely empty. They barely had time to position themselves flat against the wall before the air in front of them began to shimmer.

The flickering grew more intense, there was a sudden, dazzling burst of brightness, and a soft *whump!* sound. An extremely shabby Persian carpet had materialized on the concrete floor. But instead of delivering a fat shopkeeper and pile of ceramic tiles, the only thing to arrive on the carpet was a young girl. A young girl who was wearing nothing but a few flimsy drapes and an anguished expression.

She took one look at Ash and burst into tears. 'My heartless seducer!'

Ash had turned pale. *'Leila?'*

The girl collapsed into full-blown hysterics, simultaneously managing to beat her breast while clutching her hair and wailing. Fran, utterly confused, but horrified by the picture of misery before her, automatically moved to offer some comfort –

like a sisterly arm around her shoulder, or a sooth-ing pat, perhaps. Ash, however, grabbed her arm before she could get there. 'Stay back,' he hissed, 'she's armed and she's dangerous.'

The wailing stopped and their visitor raised her face to look at them again. She was the picture of wounded innocence, with huge misty dark eyes, honeyed skin and ripe, soft lips. Midnight dark hair tumbled around her shoulders, glittering jewels dripped from every limb. Her voice was low and sweet and throbbing.

'How can you say that, Ashazrahim? After you crushed my proffered love like mud beneath your heel! Cast me aside as if I were some flea-bitten cur who cringed before your feet!'

'Oh my God,' said Fran slowly as the truth dawned, 'it's your ex-girlfriend . . .'

'The one who turned me into a genie and impris-oned me in a ring for the last few hundred years – yes,' said Ash.

'What do you mean, a few hundred years?' the girl said with asperity. All trace of tears abruptly vanished. 'I made the curse on the Sultan's last birthday, so you've only had a year or so of enslave-ment. And you should know –' menacingly – 'I am still *extremely* vexed about the whole affair!'

'But you've travelled through time, you see,' Fran tried to explain. 'Really, Ash has been punished enough. He's a completely different person.'

Ash flinched, but Leila merely bestowed Fran with a sorrowing smile. 'Ah, now I see it all: you must be the one who let him out of the ring. Poor, deluded, unhappy child! What sleepless nights, what heartbreak awaits!'

Unhappy *child*? Leila could only be a year or two older than Fran at most! Fran clenched her right hand protectively, feeling the ring nudge into her flesh. 'I'll take the risk.'

Leila swept on as if she hadn't heard her. 'And to add insult to injury, there I was on my way to a refreshing dip in the bathhouse, only to find some scumbag attempting to remove my wall tiles with a chisel!'

'Most Gracious and Honoured Lady,' croaked Ash, now a delicate shade of green, 'there has clearly been a terrible mistake. I can explain. And apologise. And make it up to you.'

'I should think so too,' said Leila, rearranging her drapes and pouting. 'When I beat your fat friend to his getaway carpet, the last thing I expected was to be transported back into the arms of the cad who seduced and abandoned me. It has all been *most* traumatic. So you can start by conveying me out of this dung-hole of a dungeon into a suitable reception area – something with plenty of rose petals and scatter cushions.'

'Revered Princess, your wish is my command.' Ash bowed very low, then hastened to unlock the door.

'What are you doing? This is mad!' Fran managed to mutter in his ear. 'Can't you just send her back where she came from?'

'She's a Mistress of the Dark Arts,' he hissed back. 'Going along with her whims is our only chance. Believe me.'

But once Leila had been respectfully ushered into the main room, things did not go any better. 'What a poky little shop,' she exclaimed, curling her lip. 'Even the kebab stalls in the bazaar have more class.'

'Ash is doing very well for himself, actually,' said Fran, forgetting her own misgivings in defence of her boyfriend's business skills.

Leila's attention had passed to one of the glass cabinets by the window. She gave a gasp of outrage. 'Why, that's my moonstone pendant – it's been missing for *ages*. Five maids were flogged and still no one could find it.' She marched over and tried to open the case. When it proved resistant, she picked up the bronze desk lamp and calmly smashed it open, then reached through the glass to collect the jewellery. An alarm began to sound.

'I assume the oaf I found breaking and entering my bathhouse is one of your associates,' she continued, raising her voice above the bell.

'No! Well, yes. But believe me, I had no idea of Oronames's criminal tendencies. I would never, *ever* condone—'

Leila acted as if she hadn't heard (which wasn't entirely surprising, given the alarm's incessant beeping). 'So as well as a two-faced arrogant swine you're a thief too.' She picked up the desk lamp again and moved on to the next case. 'My brother's third wife's crystal perfume bottle! Just *wait* until the imperial guard find out about this.'

'One moment, if you please—' Ash was fiddling with an electronic keypad set in the wall.

'If *I* please? If *you* beg more like. Turn that noise

off and abase yourself before me.' She stamped her foot. 'At once.'

The alarm's tone had increased to a full-on wail. Ash shot her a harassed look. 'What do you think I'm trying to do? If you'll just shut up for a moment and let me—'

Leila's response was to throw the perfume bottle at his head. It missed, so she reached for an ivory chess piece instead. This one caught Ash on the shoulder and he gave a yelp of pain. Fran had had enough. She snatched up the desk lamp and stood in front of Ash, wielding it in what she hoped was a threatening manner. 'Leave him ALONE!'

'Well, well, well,' came a voice behind them, '*Reservoir Dogs* meets A Night at the Panto.'

It was Zara, who had come in unnoticed through the main door and was surveying the scene with undisguised glee. A scantily dressed foreign chick stood amidst wrecked cases and thousands of pounds' worth of antiques, while Fran waved an offensive weapon above her head and her wild-eyed boyfriend struggled to disarm the security system. She didn't have a clue what was going on, but she knew trouble when she saw it. A-grade trouble, premium class.

The next moment the alarm switched off. In the sudden silence, Fran could hear her heart pounding in her ears. Ash was visibly trembling. Leila, however, had regained her poise with the same efficiency with which she'd got over her crying fit, and was looking Zara up and down in an assessing sort of way.

'Please, Zara,' said Fran desperately, 'you have to get out of here. Really, just go.'

'*At once.*' Ash began to steer her back out of the door. 'And I would urge you to—'

Zara held her ground. 'Pipe down, Aladdin. I don't want to have anything to do with you and your 'urges'. Anyway, it seems like the fun's only just getting started. Aren't you going to introduce me to Her Royal High Turkish Delight?'

'You should learn to keep your harem under control, Ashazrahim.' Leila was still looking over Zara's black corset top, dangerously ripped denim mini and spiky black boots. 'Though your tastes have got more exotic since I saw you last. A barbarian horde seems to be missing its mascot.'

Zara raised an eyebrow. 'Oh, so you *do* speak English. That's an improvement on the last bunch of dancing bimbos Ash entertained us with. Can you do that trick when you pop a grape out of your belly button?'

'No,' replied Leila coolly, 'but I can arrange to have a girl sawn in half and her intestines pulled out through her eyeballs.'

'Maybe you should save the threats for when you're not running around in your lingerie.' Zara was smiling: it wasn't often that she found such a worthy opponent.

'I am warning you—'

'Yeah? So what are you gonna do – turn me into a kebab?'

'Zara, SHUT UP –' But Fran and Ash's simultaneous plea came too late. Leila's eyes flashed, then she flung out a bejewelled hand and snapped out something in Old Arabic. On such occasions one might expect thunder and lightning, or at least a dash of dry ice, but there was merely a loud pop. And suddenly Zara wasn't there any more.

'No!' Fran let out a cry of horror. 'No!'

'What's all the fuss?' said Leila, tossing her hair. 'I would have thought you'd be pleased to be rid of such a disagreeable harpy.'

'B-b-but w-w-what have you *done* to her?' croaked Fran, casting around in vain for signs of Zara. Not so much as a nose stud could be seen.

'I know exactly what she's done.' Ash drew himself up to his full height and his eyes glittered feverishly. 'And she is going to undo it, right now. It's time you stopped playing God, my lady.'

'Playing God? Hah! And to think there was a time when I was your One True Goddess, your Fragrant Bloom of Paradise!' Two spots of red appeared on Leila's cheeks. 'Don't you *dare* take the moral high ground, Ashazrahim. You may have pulled the wool over the eyes of Little Miss Hopelessly Devoted here, but you can't fool me.'

'Leave Fran out of it.' Ash added something very angry, in Arabic. This time it was Fran's turn to put a restraining arm on his shoulder, but he shook her off. 'No,' he said sternly, 'it's time someone took a stand. She can't get away with this.'

'Oh yes I can,' said Leila sweetly.

There was another loud pop and, like Zara, Ash vanished. This time, however, there was something else in his place: a large black cat with a bewildered expression. Fran let out a wail of despair and sank to her knees.

'Don't cry, you silly girl! Honestly, you'll learn to thank me – at least this way he can be properly domesticated.' Fran continued to quiver and gasp. Leila shrugged, then made her way to the back room, where she sketched a strange symbol in the air above the carpet. At once, it began to shrink down to the size of a small handkerchief, which she briskly tucked away among her drapery before returning to the main door. 'You must live in barbarian times,' she announced. 'The air here is foul and the buildings surpassingly ugly. Still, the scale of the place is impressive, at least. I might as well have a weekend's sightseeing before returning home.' The princess rearranged her veil and prepared to set off. 'By the way,' she said over her shoulder, 'you can keep the genie.'

Fran didn't know how long she stayed there, frozen to the spot in horror. She was past the point of thought, let alone action. After a while, however, she became dimly aware of a pain in her leg. It increased sharply. The cat had put out its paw and scratched her.

'Sorry,' it said apologetically, 'but we can't stay here all day.'

She looked back at it through a blur of tears. 'A-A-Ash?' she quavered.

'Well, my name sure ain't Felix.'

'B-b-but I thought . . . you can *speak* . . .'

'So it would appear.'

'Right. I see. Could be worse then.' Fran closed her eyes and began rocking back and forth. 'Oh God.'

'You've gone into shock,' said the cat – Ash – in conversational tones. 'Only natural. I'm feeling quite shaken up myself . . . though having gone through a similar transformation in times past does seem to lessen the impact.'

Listening to Ash's voice, with her eyes squeezed shut, it was as if nothing had changed. Fran could see him quite clearly in her head: his cool black eyes, the aristocratic arch of his nose, the dazzle of his smile. When she opened her eyes again it seemed all the more impossible to be staring into the face of a cat. Admittedly, Ash made a very handsome feline: large, black and sleek-looking. The cat bent to push its head under her arm and she flinched at the touch of its – his – fur. She couldn't help it. It was all so *wrong* . . . She got up abruptly.

'This can't be happening. Not to us, not now, after everything . . .' From being numb with shock, Fran could feel the rage bubbling up inside her. 'I am going to *kill* that witch.'

At the mention of Leila, Ash's hackles rose and his tail lashed. However, when he spoke his voice was relatively calm. 'Tempting though it is, violence is not the answer. At least not yet. As long as Leila's still in London we've got a chance to persuade her to reverse the spell.' He began to pad about restively. 'She's hysterical and vindictive, but her mood swings as rapidly as the weather round here. Which means she might be open to persuasion – especially as she took a bit of a shine to you.'

'She did?'

'Well, you're still in human form, aren't you?

And even if she is intent on staying the Fount of All Evil, we are not without resources.'

Fran frowned. 'But Leila's taken the carpet—'

'I'm talking about the genie.' She looked blank, and he flicked his tail impatiently. 'Zara, remember? Unless I'm very much mistaken, your ferocious friend is currently the new Slave of the Ring.'

'Oh.' Fran stared at the ring on her finger. There was indeed a purple glint in its depths that she hadn't seen for a very long time. 'Poor Zara,' she whispered.

'If it wasn't for "poor Zara" we probably wouldn't be in this mess. No – don't go trying to summon her up, for God's sake! There's a limit to the number of vengeful banshees I can cope with in the space of one hour . . . She'll be fine where she is for the moment. We need to come up with a plan, of course, but in the meantime the best thing for you to do is to carry on as normal. And you can start by cleaning up. I think I deactivated the alarm in time, but we don't want to draw any more attention to ourselves.'

Fran sighed. Metamorphosis clearly hadn't affected Ash's bossy streak. He was very thorough with his directions, even dictating the voicemail message she left on the phone to announce the shop was closed for stocktaking. But as she fetched a dustpan and brush to sweep up the glass, picked up the scattered treasures and generally did her best to put the place to rights, she had to admit it was rather calming to concentrate on simple tasks. And it turned out that there was at least one tangible remainder of Zara – they found her bag where she'd dumped it at the entrance.

It felt as if they'd been battling the forces of evil for an entire day, but in fact it was only just three o'clock when Fran locked up the shop and set off for home. Their departure was further delayed by the need to find a suitable mode of transportation for Ash: the only bag large enough was the one for Fran's sport kit and Ash could only be coaxed into it after much grumbling. He was a good deal heavier too than the rumpled tracksuit and mouldering trainers that usually lived there.

Once they were out in public, Ash insisted the bag was left unzipped to let some air into the sock-scented darkness, but if any of their fellow passengers noticed there was a cat on the tube, they proceeded to ignore the irregularity in the time-honoured commuter tradition. Fran sank back into her seat and tried not to think of anything at all, to force her brain into total blankness, but little shoots of panic kept breaking out. True, she was once more in possession of a genie and a ring that gave its owner seven wishes. But seeing as the effects of each wish only lasted for seven hours, she didn't see how much good it would do anyone. Helping Zara come to terms with the wacko supernatural stuff would be bad enough – breaking the news that she was supposed to obey Fran's every whim didn't bear thinking about . . .

She opened the door to the house to find a barrier constructed from a drying rack and Mickey's toy wigwam erected across the stairs. Beth must be playing Queen of the Castle again. 'Hello, love,' said Mrs Roper, coming out of the lounge. 'Enjoy the film?'

'Er, yeah. Yeah, it was good, thanks.'

She attempted to clamber past the wigwam, sports bag cradled in her arms, but she had reckoned without Beth, who emerged at the last minute from under a tea towel and launched herself at her legs. 'Kitty! Me wants kitty cat!'

Mrs Roper laughed indulgently. 'No, Beth, let Fran go past, there's a good girl. There's no ki –' She broke off. 'Good Lord, she's right! Fran – there's a *cat* in your bag.'

Beth's sticky hands were outstretched to the opening flap, from which a furry black ear was clearly visible. Silently cursing, Fran tried to raise the bag over her head and out of her sister's grasp, with the result that Ash tipped out on to the stairs and streaked up and away towards her bedroom. Beth set off in hot pursuit, but this time it was Fran's turn to block the exit route. 'Sorry, Beth,' she said breathlessly, 'but the kitty doesn't want to play.'

Her mother looked at her in bewilderment. 'But. Fran, what is that animal *doing* here?'

'It's not mine,' Fran assured her. 'I'm looking after it for a . . . for Ash. It's Ash's cat.'

'So why can't Ash look after it?'

Fran's head throbbed. 'He's, er, had to go away for a while.'

'What, today? That's rather sudden.'

'Yeah . . . family stuff.'

'Oh dear,' said her mum. 'Poor Ash. But I *do* think dumping his cat on you at the last minute is a bit much! I mean, looking after somebody else's pet is a big responsibility. Is it even house-trained?'

'Absolutely!' Fran babbled. 'It's exceptionally house-trained. A real wonder cat! And very independent – it won't get in your way or anything. I'll just go and give it a, er, cat biscuit and then I have to get down to work. Incredibly important work! In private! So please don't disturb.'

She bounded up the stairs two at a time and rushed into her bedroom, where she found Ash sitting on her bed and cleaning his whiskers.

'I hope you were joking about the cat biscuit,' he remarked. 'Just because I'm in feline form doesn't mean I'm going to be fobbed off with dead mice and vitamin pellets. In fact –' he added sighing – 'copious comfort eating may be the only way I'm going to get through this. Have you got any chocolate?'

'Maybe later,' said Fran distractedly, locking the door and going to turn on her radio, a strategy used in times past when she needed to disguise the fact she was chatting to an invisible friend. 'Look, the Leila Factor aside, I think we really do have to summon Zara out of the ring and try to explain things. I feel awful for her. She must be absolutely terrified.'

'Let's hope so,' said Ash. 'Maybe that way she'll be more cooperative. In my case, I served my first hundred commanders in a vengeful rage and the next hundred in a monumental sulk. Luckily, by the time I met you I was a paragon of sweet-tempered docility.'

This wasn't quite how Fran would have put it, but she let it pass. It was true Zara had every right to be mad as hell. And Ash had a point: although the Slave of the Ring wasn't technically allowed to harm his or her owner, Fran was sure Zara would do her best to make sure she wasn't the only one suffering . . . Fran's heart thudded uncomfortably as she began the process to activate the ring: two twists forward, one twist back.

Once again, the purple jewel began to gleam, throwing its brightness into the air before her, which flared and flickered in turn. The light faded into a purplish haze that rapidly – all too rapidly – gathered shape and solidity. In a matter of seconds, Zara was standing in the room, large as life and twice as terrifying.

'Not even so much as a *thunderbolt*!' she spat. 'I can't sodding believe it!'

Instinctively, Ash and Fran both took a step back. Purplish black smoke coiled from under the heels of Zara's boots; the spikes in her hair were practically bristling with rage. A thick metal bracelet now encircled her upper arm, its runes faintly glowing with the same power that gleamed within the ring. She advanced across the room with her teeth bared in a wolfish snarl.

'No, I mean it – what's the point of having magic powers if I'm not allowed to blast anyone to smithereens? Starting with the two goons who got me into this mess.'

'Oh, Zara!' Fran had tears in her eyes. 'I'm so, so sorry. But between the three of us, you know, I'm sure we'll find some way to get you back to normal. And you're not the only one Leila magicked. Ash—'

'Mr Cuddles here, I know.' Zara gave him a black look. 'Seems like one curse victim can spot another.'

'So you understand what's happened to you? About the, er, genie-fication?'

'Clear as crystal balls. That witch even arranged for two-metre-high letters of flame to spell it out for me – horrible gloating cow.' She turned to Ash. 'So I guess this is the key to your mystery past?'

'You assume correctly, O Accursed and Unfortunate Lady,' replied Ash, who tended to revert to hyperbole when he was nervous. 'I was banged up in the ring for several centuries.'

'Bleeding hell.' She brooded for a while. 'Do you know what the scariest thing is? I'm not even expecting to wake up and find this is all some spaced-out hallucination. A lot of freakish stuff went on just before you arrived on the scene, and now it sort of makes *sense*.' She looked at Ash again. 'Hah! I always knew there was something dodgy about you. Apart from the girlie shirts and mooning over Fran, of course. So the question is: how did you get out of this trinket?'

There was a pause.

'Fran kissed me.'

There was another pause, an even longer one. Then, 'Eurrrrrgh! You have *got* to be kidding. There's no way I'm snogging Fran, not even for fifty thunderbolts.'

'Yeah well,' Fran muttered, 'that was different. It was . . . a . . . a matter of the heart.'

'Matter of the heart my arse. After a century or two cooped up in a ring, your handsome prince must have been well and truly gagging for it.' Zara sneered. 'Give me a few years at this lark and I'm guessing I won't be too fussy either.'

Fran, though she had turned bright red, wasn't going to take this. 'Look, Zara, I know you've had a horrible shock. But there's no point blaming us. *Leila* is the villain here. So if you're going to get out of that ring, and Ash is to return to human form, we're all going to have to work together.'

'Suddenly life as a cat doesn't seem so bad,' growled Ash, whose hackles were raised.

Zara ignored him. 'OK, fine. First, let's get a couple of things straight. One, I'm not taking any of that mistress/slave rubbish, whatever that bitch may have magicked into my contract. This is going to be a working partnership, except for the fact I'll be a lot more senior than you two, cos I'm the one with the Harry Potter powers. So show a little respect.'

Fran tried to look humble. She knew from her experience with Ash that being the Commander of the Ring involved a lot more soothing and coaxing than giving orders. He'd once told her that granting a wish was all about 'visualization', whatever that was supposed to mean, but wouldn't be drawn into specifics, saying that all trades had their secrets. One thing was clear, however: although a genie was duty-bound to grant its owner's wishes, this didn't mean he or she was without ways of helping a wish-fulfilment to go unpleasantly wrong.

'And two, there isn't going to be *any* kind of further negotiation until someone gets me a fag.'

'But I don't smoke . . . and . . . there aren't any—'

'Yes there are,' put in Ash grudgingly. 'There was a packet of cigarettes in Zara's bag. You brought it along, didn't you?' His furry shoulders hunched in a shrug. 'When it comes to the genie–client relationship, a little TLC can go a long way.'

'Too right, Cat Boy,' said Zara approvingly. 'Next time around, I'll have a double vodka and coke.'

Fran reluctantly passed a cigarette to her new genie. 'If you wouldn't mind doing that out of the window . . .' She trailed off as Zara lit the cigarette with a snap of her fingers and inhaled luxuriously, floating a couple of metres up into the air as she did so. She sprawled on her side, bobbing gently, and blew a plume of smoke into Fran's eyes.

'Hmm, this is kind of cool. Maybe this gig has its perks after all . . . OK, so what's the plan?'

A good question. Tentatively Fran explained that Ash thought they should have a shot at persuading Leila to change her mind and that, if she wouldn't, she might provide some sort of clue as to how they could go about undoing the spells for themselves. So their first priority was to find Leila. It was, of course, a risk: she might still be so angry she'd take one look at Fran and turn her into a cross-eyed camel. Then there was the problem that Leila could be literally anywhere – who knew if she was even in the same time and space dimension? But it was a starting point.

Four cigarettes later, and after much bickering, a carefully worded wish had been chosen. Fran had just opened her mouth to say, 'Please, Zara, would you kindly transport me to wherever Leila is so that I can talk to her without endangering myself or others,' when she realized her mum was shouting at her from the stairs.

'FRAN – some boy is here to see you!'

'WHAT?' Fran bawled, turning down the radio but not moving to unlock the door. Although Zara was invisible to everyone except the ring's owner and her fellow curse-victim, the cloud of cigarette smoke she'd generated was not.

'A BOY I said! To SEE YOU! Says it's IMPORTANT! Think his name's FINN!'

Quinn? Since when were Quinn and Fran on visiting terms? Zara's eyebrows were raised so high they practically disappeared into her hair spikes. Ash-the-cat was sitting bolt upright, his whiskers bristling.

'Look, I'd better go and get rid of him,' Fran said apologetically. 'I don't know why he's here, but he probably just wants to moan about Francesca. Give me two secs –'

Zara was about to launch into something abusive, but Fran remembered in time that two twists of the ring would send the genie back where she came from. Ash was less easy to get rid of, since the moment she opened the door he slipped past her legs like black smoke. She just hoped he'd remember to keep his mouth shut.

Fran followed her mum downstairs to find Quinn already settled at the kitchen table, her little sister in attendance. 'Hello, nice boy!' Beth burbled. Quinn flashed her the smile that used to send the female population of Conville Secondary into a collective swoon.

'What are you doing here?' Fran asked flatly. Had

this vision of alpha-male adorability appeared in her kitchen six weeks or so ago, she would probably be joining Beth for a spot of burbling. Right now, however, all she wanted was to get rid of him.

Quinn hung his head. 'I'm sorry, Fran, I – I – just kind of need somebody to talk to at the moment. But if you want me to go . . .'

'Well, yeah, actually. I'm afraid it's not a good time.'

'Nonsense!' Mrs Roper could hardly believe her ears. 'Where're your manners?' she hissed. 'The least you can do is offer the poor boy a cup of tea. Come on, Beth, it's time for your bath.' She picked up a protesting Beth and bustled out of the room.

For a moment it looked as if nobody was going to say anything. Meanwhile, Ash had jumped up on to the table and was fixing Quinn with a sinister stare.

'Nice cat,' Quinn said at last, moving to stroke it. Ash promptly scratched the offending hand with a swipe of his paw. 'Jesus!'

'Yeah, sorry about that. He can be very temperamental . . . Look, I don't mean to be rude, but is there any particular reason you wanted to see me? It's just I'm about to go out, and . . .'

His eyes had never looked so darkly brooding. 'I don't blame you, you know. I've been a horrible heartless git and there's no reason for you to give me the time of day. But –' pleadingly – 'I want to change. I've spent the last few weeks working out where I went wrong, and what I should do to fix it.' He took a deep breath. 'You see, I've decided I don't want to be shallow any more.'

So this was the rationale behind the shaven locks and shunned groupies! 'That's, er, great. But I don't see what I've got to do with it. Surely your mates . . . I mean, we don't even know each other that well, do we?'

Quinn had the grace to look abashed. Fran was two years younger and until recently had just been another star-struck schoolkid: Francesca's frumpy friend. However, the new, reformed Quinn was beginning to realize he had underestimated Fran. The way she had listened earlier, outside school, for example: so sensitive and sympathetic! He'd always thought she was rather sweet, but now there was an edge to her – brusque, confident – that was very intriguing. She had blossomed and, what's more, had a boyfriend to prove it . . . He made his voice as low and chocolatey as possible. 'I'm not asking for a lot – just a bit of guidance really. To help me be a better person.'

'Fine,' said Fran distractedly. Ash had begun yowling, and was prowling up and down the table in a menacing sort of way. 'But now I'm afraid you really must leave.'

'No worries.' Quinn got to his feet. 'You off to meet your boyfriend again?'

'Yes. No. He's had to go away for a while –' Suddenly she was looking a little shifty. In fact, she was practically hustling him out of the door.

Interesting, thought Quinn.

Once Quinn was out of the way, Ash and Zara were free to voice their displeasure. 'I thought we had an agreement,' Zara snarled the moment she was recalled from the ring. 'What happened to all that touchy-feely teamwork crud? I'm not some freakin' radio station you can switch off when it suits you.' Meanwhile, Ash was still bridling at Fran's tolerance towards 'the dung-beetle blond' and became even moodier when she refused to take him along to her interview with Leila. 'Everything about you makes her mad,' she reasoned, 'and we have to face the fact that in your current form it's not like you can do much anyway.' Ash accepted the first point, but it took a lot more arguing to convince him of the second.

At least the granting of the wish was straightforward: a tingle, a purplish blur and the jolt of the stomach you get just as a roller coaster descends. Though it did seem a bit of a waste of a wish to open her eyes and find herself outside a wine bar only a couple of streets away from Oronames's shop. Fran's stomach did another jolt, this time one of panic. She found places like this intimidating at the best of times: the place was dim and smoky, the clientele mostly middle-aged males. And a psychotic time-travelling witch, watching the television screen in the corner.

Hovering by the door, Fran tried to recall the various delicate and complicated things Ash had told her to say and instead found herself hoping that the bar manager would take one look at her schoolgirl face and eject her before she got within hexing distance. In theory, her wish had been worded so that she would be protected from a sudden blast of Dark Arts, but Zara was a very inexperienced genie. An inexperienced genie who hated her guts . . . It was not so much courage as helplessness that finally propelled her through the door and over to Leila's table. 'Um, excuse me—' she began.

'Oh, hello again.' Leila dragged her eyes away from the TV, which was showing a repeat of *Hype!*, with Posy Parkin flirting outrageously with a Hollywood film star. 'I assume you're here to abase yourself at my feet and beg for mercy on behalf of Ashazrahim the Despicable, Scum of Arabia and Halfwit of Baghdad. Am I right?'

'Er, pretty much.'

'In that case, I'm sure you could do with some refreshment.' Leila clicked her fingers at a small bald man who'd been hovering at an admiring distance. 'We'll have another two of those jinn tonics,' she told him imperiously. She leaned towards Fran in a confiding manner. 'Apparently, all I have to do is promise to give him my number! Tell me, will any number do or should it possess some kind of mystic or mathematical significance? It seems a very strange system of bartering . . .'

Fran gulped. She saw Leila had exchanged her flowing silks for a blue blazer of the type favoured by middle-aged bankers, worn over the type of floral nightgown favoured by their wives. Her flowing black locks were piled on her head and tied in place with what looked suspiciously like a polka-dot tea towel. Together with the ropes of gems glittering at her neck and wrists, the effect was eccentric but weirdly cool. It was the sort of outfit a fashion student might throw together for a little light posing down the Portobello Road.

'Time travelling incognito is *such* fun,' Leila

blithely continued. 'I can't think why I haven't done it before! Though I was very fortunate to find someone willing to part with their merchandise, otherwise goodness knows how I would have managed my disguise.' So that's where the tea-towel-and-blazer ensemble came from! Fran saw that there were, in fact, several bags at Leila's feet, one of which was filled with jars of olive oil and truffle sauce, and another with a child's swimming costume. Fran wondered what had happened to the original owner of the shopping, and how 'willing' the handover had really been.

'But can't you just, um, magic up anything you want?' she asked, curious in spite of herself.

'Gracious, no. Really, my resources are very modest – just a few bits and bobs I like to keep around in case of emergency. This amulet here, for example –' she fingered a small black pebble hanging from a ribbon around her neck – 'is a family heirloom from the Tower of Babel. Its powers of translation have proved remarkably useful.' That would explain the fluent English. 'And then there's my curse bracelet of course.'

'Curse bracelet?'

'Like a charm bracelet. Only the trinkets are used to inflict misfortune, rather than bring luck. There's a little bottle for poisoning, a gargoyle for demonic possession and so on. Very dinky.'

'I see.' Fran cleared her throat nervously. 'About that cursing thing . . .'

'Oh, you're not *still* going on about the whole turning-your-boyfriend-into-a-cat business! And surely even you would agree that nightmare harpy got no more than she deserved . . . Of course, I realize Ashazrahim's new form may take a little getting used to, but once you've calmed down and got things into perspective I think you'll find I've done you a favour. You see – 'she said with sorrowful sigh, and a confiding smile – 'I like you, Fran. I don't want you to suffer as I did. After all, we're both victims of cruel, deceitful men.'

'I am no victim and Ash has paid for his wrongdoings,' said Fran quietly. 'The only cruelty here is what you did to Zara and him this afternoon.'

There was an unpleasant silence. Fran somehow managed to hold Leila's stare, although every instinct was screaming at her to get out and away while she still could. *Please*, she prayed, *please* . . .

'Such blind devotion!' the princess said at last. 'Female emancipation clearly has a long way to go. Still, your obstinacy is oddly touching. Perhaps I *was* a little hasty.'

Fran's heart was leaping about so hard she felt could barely breathe. 'So you – you will agree to undo the curses?'

Leila shrugged. 'Unfortunately, it's impossible.' Fran let out a groan of despair. 'You see, the thing is, once a curse has been cast I keep its power locked up safe in one of those cute little trinket things. My curse bracelet, remember? To destroy the source of the power you have to destroy the whole bracelet, and the complete set of charms. And I'm afraid I got rid of them all this afternoon.'

'Got rid – but – why – how—'

'I exchanged the bracelet for these clothes and things,' she said airily. 'I purchased them from a little girl waiting for her mother outside a covered bazaar. She drove a hard bargain, I must say. Mind you, I didn't see any reason why I would ever need to reverse the spells. It seemed a reasonable exchange at the time.'

'OK, but can't I just use a wish to get the bracelet back?' Fran's voice swelled with hope.

'Well, yes, but that wouldn't be much good because, even if you destroyed it, it would return to its original form after seven hours, and disappear again.'

Fran put her head in her hands.

'Cheer up – I'm sure it can't have gone too far. Think of it as a quest, like the heroes go on! Very character building, I believe, and *lots* of fun.

'Now, the destruction ritual: first you wash it in the blood of a black stallion. Fast for seven days and seven nights, then place the charms in an ivory casket bound with three strands of a murderer's hair and bury it under a cypress tree at midnight. Finally all you need to do is chant the relevant incantations – how good is your Babylonian, by the way?'

Fran just stared.

'Never mind. If you're pressed for time, you can always stamp on it three times with your left foot. Not so much fun, but apparently just as effective . . . Tell me,' Leila said, pointing to the television screen, 'is that the queen of these parts?'

'Goddess, according to some people,' said Fran morosely, remembering what Naz had said. Posy's carefree laughter seemed to be mocking her from inside the screen.

'Truly?'

'Well, not literally. She's just very popular. She and this other person, Zed, present a chat show . . . Basically, she gets paid to wear great clothes and flirt with celebrities all day.'

'I see the mob pay her great homage,' Leila commented as the camera panned back to show the cheering studio audience. Her face brightened. 'Tell you what, before you go do you want to try one of these cocktail thingies? I really can't see why the tail of a chicken should be very appetizing . . . but there's no point going on holiday unless you're willing to sample new things!'

Fran didn't get home until late. Leila had been very reluctant to see her leave – 'We girls must stick together!' – and embraced her tenderly on parting. Fran hadn't dared enquire what her plans were for the next few days, or how she was going to support herself in London, but she supposed a Mistress of the Dark Arts was more than capable of looking after herself.

She reported back to the others in the tiny shed at the bottom of the Roper's garden. It was a hide-out from Ash's genie days, when the two of them would share a tub of chocolate spread and he'd berate her for being a snivelling female and she'd accuse him of being a chauvinist git . . . Fran got quite misty-eyed at the memory. However, they took the news better than she'd expected.

'We knew this wasn't going to be easy,' said Ash, 'and, frankly, it could be a lot worse. First thing in the morning we'll spend a wish to track down the kid and grab the goods. This time tomorrow it could all be over.'

Hmm. Maybe he was right and all it would take would be a little light wish-making, then hey presto and happily ever after. But if Fran's previous experience was anything to go by, magical things were rarely that simple. There were practical considerations, too – what would Zara's family do when she didn't come home that night? And what if they didn't wrap things up in the next day or so? Ash's absence could be explained without much fuss but AWOL schoolgirls were a different matter. Especially if she'd last been seen having a row in a smashed-up antiques shop with Fran and her mysterious Iraqi boyfriend, who had also vanished . . . Next stop, *Crimewatch*.

Zara found this prospect highly amusing – 'Serve you two cretins right if you make 'Britain's Most Wanted' – until Fran pointed out she could hardly set about undoing the curse if she spent the next week being interrogated in a police cell. Since Zara was meant to be spending the weekend with her dad, the best they could do was to send a text from Zara's mobile to Mr Truman, informing him that something had come up and she couldn't make it. Since Zara's parents weren't on speaking terms, and lived on different sides of the city, they should be covered for the next couple of days. In theory.

When Fran finally tumbled into bed, she felt dizzy with exhaustion but too wired to fall asleep. All she could think of was Ash, Leila, Zara . . . Leila, Zara, Ash . . . round and round in her head like a nightmare merry-go-round. Finally, she turned on the light and got up to pace around the room for a while. On the pinboard facing the bed was a snap-shot of her and Ash that Amira had taken in the park one weekend. He had caught her round the waist and was wearing a silly grin on his face; she was laughing as her hair blew into his eyes. Two people born into different worlds, centuries apart, an Arabian prince and a London schoolgirl, and yet – somehow – there they were: an ordinary couple, fooling around on an ordinary afternoon. Fran gave herself a shake. 'I swear,' she said aloud to the photo, 'I'm going to get us back.'

In spite of the determined and defiant thoughts with which she'd gone to sleep, when Fran woke up the next morning it took a while to remember that this was no ordinary Saturday. She lay relaxed for a few drowsy moments, then shot upright, cold with dread. Of course. How could she have forgotten?

She found Ash in the kitchen, surveying a saucer of milk with distaste. 'There you are,' he said grumpily. 'I thought you were never going to get up. It's nearly nine.'

Fran didn't usually get up before eleven on a Saturday but this was not a normal weekend. They had a heavy day of questing ahead. She was surprised to see that the table bore signs that the rest of the family had already breakfasted – apparently she wasn't the only one with an early start. 'Where is everyone?'

'Your mum was just here. Your dad and Mickey left half an hour ago – apparently he's due at the photographer's studio today. Something about a shoot for the Kookie campaign.'

Fran's little brother was something of a household name, after being recruited by a child talent agency to advertise everything from toilet spray to fish fingers. His latest project was the launch of a new kind of cake bar. Fran rubbed her gritty eyes and yawned extravagantly. 'Well, I know we've got forces of evil to battle and all that, but I could murder a Kookie cake right now. How about some breakfast?'

'Now you're talking.'

Fran was busy preparing Ash a light snack of toasted bagels, peanut butter and jam when her mother came in, hunting for her mobile.

'Hello, love, you're up early! Mmm, that looks good.'

'Ash's favourite,' she said unthinkingly. She had cut half the bagel into bite-sized pieces and arranged them on a saucer. 'The cat, I mean. Ash the cat.'

'Your boyfriend named his cat after *himself*?'

'No, of course not,' said Fran feebly. 'The cat's name is . . . um . . . Cuddles.'

Ash hissed and Mrs Roper gave him a startled look. 'Doesn't Cuddles eat cat food, then?'

'No,' she said firmly. 'He's got a very delicate appetite. Ash always feeds him from his own plate.'

'Nothing but the best for His Lordship.' Her mum gave a slightly strained laugh. Fran suspected she wasn't referring to the cat.

So it was just as well she hadn't found the nest Fran had made out of her best pashmina for 'Cuddles' in the utility room, where Mrs Roper insisted he was shut up for the night. Not that Ash was acting particularly grateful for his bed, or his breakfast, or Fran's offer to make him a bespoke collar out of a diamanté choker of hers he'd always liked. She knew his bad mood was in part a delayed reaction to the traumatic events of yesterday, but when Zara stormed out of the ring in her customary huff of smoke, Fran felt tempted to see if Leila was still up for a bit of bar crawling.

The main bone of contention was Fran's resolve to accomplish the next wish without either of the others around to distract her. Ash was insistent that he come along, if only for moral support, but Fran, who had already had quite enough of explaining why she was carrying her boyfriend's cat around in a bag, didn't really see the point. 'It's not as if we're going to have the time and opportunity for spontaneous pep talks.'

'Exactly,' put in Zara, who was equally determined not to be left out of things. 'That's why you don't want a nattering fur ball but a light-fingered genie at your side. I can nick the bracelet without anyone being any the wiser.'

Fran brightened at this, but Ash was shaking his head. 'You and the bracelet are made from the same magic,' he told her, 'and as such you can't have physical contact. At best, you'd get your fingers burned. At worst, your two powers would cancel each other out. Permanently.'

Zara refused to be put off. 'I can still be useful! Dispensing advice, imparting wisdom, muttering threats . . . and no one else will be able to see or hear me. You can pretend you're schizophrenic or something. It'll be great.'

Neither option seemed especially great to Fran, but she tried to remind herself how frustrating it must be for the other two to have to watch from the sidelines. After all, they had more at stake then she did.

Finally, she agreed to take Ash along in the sports bag – for observational purposes only – and made a promise to let Zara out of the ring the minute she had some progress to report. Only then could she get on with the actual wish-making.

'Please, Super Mighty Goddess Zara, would you be so kind as to transport Ash and myself to wherever Leila's curse bracelet is –'

Fran blinked. She was standing in the garden of a showy modern house in a quiet suburban street. It appeared she'd arrived in the middle of preparations for a party, for most of the lawn was taken up with a pink marquee, and pink and white balloons festooned every available railing and tree. Catering staff were unloading crockery from a van parked in the drive, while two men struggled to fix a banner across the porch. The banner was emblazoned with 'Happy 10th Birthday, Darling Tallulah'.

Ash poked his furry head out of the sports bag. 'Any sign of the brat with the bling?'

'Shh!' Fran hissed, ducking behind a clump of pampas grass. 'Give me a chance – we've only just got here.'

An irritable-looking blonde woman had just come out of the house, accompanied by a younger man with a goatee. She inspected the banner and gestured to its sweating handlers that it needed lifting to the right. Then she marched towards the marquee, where an anxious young woman with a clipboard was hovering.

'I'm very sorry, Mrs Tarbuck-Smythe,' she said, 'but the agency has just phoned to say that the magician's car has a flat tyre, so he's running about twenty minutes late.'

'Well, really! That's just not good enough. I have fifty young guests arriving in an hour, and I *specifically* requested that this Mr Magnifico be on hand to greet them on arrival.'

'What a pity his powers don't extend to conjuring up a new tyre,' drawled the man with the goatee.

'If you're not going to say anything helpful, Stuart,' Mrs T-S snapped, 'I'd rather you didn't say anything at all. Poor Tallie's already *most* disappointed you're not staying for the party and—'

'Who are you?'

Fran jumped. She had been so busy eavesdropping that she hadn't realized a small girl had appeared and was staring at her suspiciously. She thought rapidly. 'Er . . . I'm the magician's assistant.'

'You don't look very magical. What's that in your bag?'

'My –? Oh, that's my cat. He's, um, part of the routine.'

'He's *gorgeous*.' Without asking, she scooped up the cat and squashed him to her chest. 'What's he called?'

'Cuddles.'

The girl smirked. 'That's a stupid name.'

Fran had to agree, though she didn't think someone entitled Tallulah Tarbuck-Smythe was in a position to criticize.

The birthday girl was a lumpish sort of kid, whose flowery name seemed at odds with her small piggy eyes and peevish expression. She was wearing a suede miniskirt, matching boots and a jumper with a white fur trim. And a tarnished metal bracelet on her left wrist.

'Tallie, precious!' the blonde woman called. 'The photographer wants to take some shots of you in front of the marquee.' She caught sight of Fran and frowned. 'Who are you and what are you doing here?'

'I'm the magician's assistant,' Fran replied with a bright smile and a sinking heart. 'Francesca the, um . . . Fantastic. I got a lift here ahead of him.'

'Nonsense – the talent agency didn't say anything about an assistant. And you only look a few years older than Tallie.'

'Look, Mummy! Look, Uncle Stuart!' Tallulah called out. 'Come and see the kitty.' She hauled Ash over her shoulder by the scruff of his neck and he made a strangled sort of sound. 'Oooh, how cute! He's purring!'

But her mother was not so easily distracted. 'Poppet, put that animal down. He's sure to be *riddled* with fleas.' Ash yowled in protest. 'Listen, Miss Whoever-you-are, I'm certainly not going to let you into this property without some kind of identification.'

'Mummy, don't be such a meanie!'

'I'm only doing this for your own safety, precious. After that dreadful, dreadful incident I could never forgive myself if anything happened to you.'

'What incident was that then?' asked Uncle Stuart, looking bored.

'The brave darling was mugged! Yes! I'd left her with the shopping for a minute when some foreign maniac came up and grabbed all our bags . . . Poor Tallulah was too traumatized to give a proper description, but I'm sure it was one of those nasty Albanian types. You know, Gypsies.' She shuddered. 'Anyway, since then my nerves have been completely shredded. You simply can't trust anyone these days.'

Stuart regarded Fran disparagingly. 'Well, she doesn't look very dangerous. Or foreign. But if you're worried you could always just phone the—'

'I'm sorry for the confusion,' said Fran quickly, 'but I'm not having you on. I really am Mr . . . Mr Magnifico's assistant. Look, I'll give you a demonstration to prove it.'

She twisted the ring and the next moment Zara materialized on the lawn – though of course only the ring-bearer could see her. Before the genie could launch into her usual tirade, Fran jerked her head in the direction of Tallulah's wrist, and raised her brows in what she hoped was a significant manner. Then she pointed toward the nearest flower bed, where a miniature stone cherub was nestling. 'Ladies and gentleman, with the help of my, er, invisible fairy friend, I'll say the magic words that will make that garden ornament disappear.'

'I'm not some kind of pink git with a sparkly wand,' the genie complained. 'Why can't I be your invisible demonic friend?'

'Luckily, my helper understands that obeying my commands is for her own good,' Fran said firmly. 'Oronames Ashazrahim hoity-toity toot!' She waved her hands in vague and supposedly mystic gestures.

Zara huffed, but stalked over to the flower bed. As soon as the genie had picked up the ornament, it vanished from ordinary view.

'Not bad,' said Tallulah.

'It's all done with mirrors of course,' said Mrs T-S.

Uncle Stuart yawned.

'And now,' Fran announced, 'I'll say the magic words that will return the cherub to my own hands. Abracadabra Ali Baba Oxymoron-ocious!'

Zara rolled her eyes, but passed the cherub over. From the three onlookers' perspective, it had materialized from thin air.

This time, Fran actually got some applause. She took a bow. 'For my final demonstration before the performance, I call upon Cuddles the Wonder Cat.' With a twist of the ring, she sent her protesting genie back where she came from, before taking Ash from Tallulah and setting him gently on the ground. 'Think of a number between one and ten,' she asked her audience, which had been joined by one of the banner handlers and a couple of waiters en route to the marquee.

'I choose four,' announced Tallulah in a regal manner.

'An excellent choice. I am going to hold up four

fingers, and Cuddles will count them for me by turning around in a circle.'

Ash obligingly turned around four times. The applause grew louder.

'And now, O Mighty and All-Knowing Wonder Cat, please can you tell us how old Tallulah is going to be today? And, er, take it slowly – we don't want you getting dizzy or anything . . .'

Ash shot her a reproachful look but walked round and round in a stately circle as his audience counted up to ten. He had to sit down rather abruptly at the end, to coos from Tallulah, a grudging smile from her mother and cheers from the rest.

'Looks like Miss Fantastic has proved herself,' Stuart drawled. He checked his watch. 'I'd better be off. I'm due at this wretched wedding reception at one and Lily's already phoned three times.'

'Oh, very well,' said Mrs T-S. 'But, really, the agency should have informed me they were sending two people; it's all *most* irregular. And I'm certainly not paying any extra. Come along, Tallie – the photographer's waiting.'

'I want to stay here with the cat,' replied her daughter ungraciously as she sat down. 'You go and I'll come along in a bit.'

She continued to stroke Ash with a pummelling sort of motion. With a last-ditch wriggle, he managed to butt his head against the bracelet dangling from Tallulah's left wrist and give a meaningful 'prrp!' in Fran's direction. She got the message.

'That's an unusual bracelet you're wearing,' Fran said at last, as casually as she could make it.

'It's nothing special,' said Tallulah dismissively.

'I thought it was cool at first, but it's not like it's even silver or anything. Daddy's getting me a proper one for my birthday. From Tiffany's.'

Fran's spirits rose. 'Can I have a look?'

It was, at first glance, just an ordinary charm bracelet: a chain made from some tarnished metal from which small pendants hung. But instead of the usual hearts and dice and ballet shoes, Fran could see, among other things, a miniature gargoyle and an axe. 'Yeah, I see what you mean,' she said, trying to sound neutral. 'It's a bit goth, isn't it?'

'That's what Uncle Stuart said.'

'The funny thing is,' she said carefully, 'I've got a fancy-dress party it would be just right for. How about I bought it off you?'

Tallulah stopped pummelling Ash's ears and regarded her coolly. 'How much?'

'I dunno, maybe a fiver . . .'

Tallulah pursed her lips.

'Ten quid then? I mean, like you said, it's not even silver . . .'

Stony silence.

'Twenty? Thirty? Er . . . fifty?'

Ash made another 'prrp!' sound. Too late: Tallulah had scented weakness. 'But it looks really old! It might be *antique*. It's probably worth *hundreds* of pounds.'

Hell's bells. Desperately Fran tried to think of something she could offer that might conceivably appeal to the brat who had everything. She failed.

'Tell you what,' said Tallulah at last, her pudgy face taking on a shrewd expression. 'I'll do you a swap. My bracelet for your cat.'

'*What?*'

'Well, a charm bracelet's to bring luck and if I give mine to you something bad might happen.' She smirked. 'Everyone knows black cats are the luckiest things ever. And I'm tired of boring old guinea pigs and that stupid rabbit.'

'But this is Cuddles the Wonder Cat! I can't do my act without him!'

Tallulah narrowed her eyes. 'No cat, no deal.'

They faced each other in silence. Fran was the first to crack. 'B-b-but won't your mum mind?' she asked feebly.

Tallulah bestowed a kiss on the top of Ash's head, then got to her feet. 'Mummy won't be a problem – she's still crippled with guilt about the mugging. Make your mind up while I'm getting my photo taken, OK?'

The moment her back was turned, Fran and Ash retreated behind the pampas grass. Ash made a retching sound and set to putting his ruffled fur to rights. 'That girl needs to learn some manners. I'm a pedigree feline, not a sack of potatoes.'

'Don't worry, there's no way I'm going to sell you to that – that monster. Can you believe she made up all that rubbish about getting robbed for the shopping? She's even more obnoxious than Leila!' Fran began to chew her nails. 'Maybe if I phone my dad and make up some cash-flow crisis . . .'

'It's me she wants, though, not the money. Apparently even in cat form I'm irresistible – joke,' he added hastily, seeing Fran's expression.

'This isn't a joke; it's a nightmare that's getting

more nightmarish by the minute. There *must* be another way of getting the bracelet back.'

'But this is the simplest one. Look, I'll stay here with the little beast, wait an hour or two, then give her the slip and hitchhike back to Milson Road – catch a lift on a milk float or something. Meanwhile, you get the bracelet and work your magic –' he thought for a moment – 'Though it might be an idea to postpone the de-cursing until I'm home and dry. I would prefer to do my transforming away from fifty over-excited ten-year-olds.'

Fran swallowed. 'If you think that's our best option . . . I just . . . I just don't want to leave you with that awful girl.'

'I know,' he said softly. 'It's like yesterday – I hated letting you go off to face Leila on your own. But you did what you had to do, and now we're a step closer to sorting everything out. So now it's my turn.' He pushed his head against her arm, but this time she didn't flinch at the touch of his fur. 'And the thing about Wonder Cats is that we *always* land on our feet.'

Ten minutes later, Tallulah marched over to where Fran was brooding. 'I've told Mummy about the cat and it's fine,' she announced. 'So if you still want the bracelet, it's time to pay up.'

'You – you – you will be kind to him?' Fran asked tremulously as she passed Ash over. Now that the moment of parting had come, Fran found it hard to keep her emotions in check. 'He's a very valuable animal, you know: top pedigree, rare Arabian breed. So you can't give him normal cat food. He loves bagels, and peanut butter, and chicken chow mein –'

Tallulah rolled her eyes. 'Whatever. Here's the bracelet.' She tossed it at Fran's feet.

Fran reached out to stroke Ash lightly on the head. 'Goodbye, Cuddles,' she managed to say. 'And – and good luck.'

'He's *my* good luck now,' said Tallulah coolly, turning away with Ash slung over her shoulder.

Fran took a few moments to compose herself behind the pampas grass. She knew she had to get going before the real magician arrived, but this was the first time she'd seen the bracelet close up. Although the charms were small, the metal was intricately detailed and glinted eerily in the light. There was the poison bottle and the gargoyle Leila had told her about, so presumably the axe was for violent death and the hand covered in lumps for plague or something . . . In which case, how were the genie and animal transformations represented? A horrible thought struck her.

She hurried over to the marquee, where she found Tallulah inspecting a six-tiered pink birthday cake. 'Er, hello again. There weren't any other charms when you first had the bracelet, were there?'

Tallulah screwed up her face. 'I s'pose there *might* have been a couple of others. One of a ring, I think, and one of some kind of animal.' Fran's heart skipped a beat. 'But it's too late now,' Tallulah added as Ash frantically squirmed in her arms. 'You can't go back on a swap once you've done the exchange. Everyone knows that. It's, like, the *rules*.'

Fran said, struggling to keep her voice calm, 'What happened to the other charms?'

Tallulah heaved a long-suffering sigh. 'I gave the

animal thingy to Daisy yesterday. And Uncle Stuart picked up the ring one, cos it snapped off. He said his girlfriend would like it.'

Fran tried to process all this new information. 'Wh-who's Daisy?'

'Daisy Adams. She used to be my second-best friend, which is why I gave her the charm, but then she went back on her promise to bring her brother to my party today. So of course I uninvited her, and now she's my third-worst enemy. Which is a shame, because Quinn is *so* the scrummiest boy in the whole wide world . . .' Her pudgy features took on a dreamy expression, which was abruptly cut short as Ash dug his claws into her back. 'Ouch!' she yelped, taking him by the scruff of his neck and giving him a shake. '*Bad* cat!'

Well, well. The one and only Quinn 'Scrummiest Boy in the World' Adams. Fran didn't know whether to be relieved or dismayed at this latest twist. But before she could quiz Tallulah further, or have any kind of last-minute communication with Ash, Mrs Tarbuck-Smythe came along to sweep daughter and cat up. 'We have to get a move-on, munchkin, if we're going to get your hair done on time!'

Fran didn't want to waste time either: she went straight over to the harassed-looking woman with the clipboard and asked where Stuart was. But here, too, luck was not on her side. Apparently Stuart had already left. 'He's had to dash off to a wedding reception, I think,' she was told. 'At the Unicorn Lounge.' Fran inwardly groaned. It was going to be a long, long day.

*

Back at home Fran's spirits were further lowered by the discovery that she had ten missed calls on her mobile, all from Amira. The Butterflies were supposed to be practising this morning, but what with one catastrophe and another, Fran found it hard to get worked up about a missed rehearsal. Unfortunately her manager was bound to see it differently.

To her relief (and surprise) Amira was more worried than raving; apparently the most recent messages she'd left had been of the slightly panicked 'are you still alive' rather than the 'you are so dead' variety. After Fran had established that, no, neither she nor anyone else in the Roper household had been hit by a bus, she did her best to convey a sense of the urgent and unexpected without going into the specifics.

'I'm really sorry, but I can't go into details, just ask you to trust me – and believe how bad I feel about letting you guys down.'

'Listen, babe, I know you're as committed to the band as the rest of us. So if what you need is to be left in peace to work whatever it is all through, then that's what you'll get, straight up. But are you sure me and the girls can't help?'

Fran paused. 'Well, now you come to mention it . . .' If she was going to be out for the rest of the day, it might be a good idea to have a cover story to account for her absence – like an intensive rehearsal session with the Butterflies, for example. Since Ash had arrived on the scene, Mr and Mrs Roper were especially keen on knowing exactly where their eldest daughter was and what she was doing, and Fran knew she'd feel safer if Amira was on standby to back her up. Although Amira was obviously dying to know what was really going on, she nobly restrained herself from asking more questions and promised to help Fran keep her story straight. 'No worries, doll. It's what a good manager is for.'

Fran felt quite emotional when she put the phone down. After battling with a psychotic witch, an obnoxious genie and a pint-sized super-brat, it was nice to come across some Girl Power of the non-toxic kind. And speaking of toxic . . .

Once released from the ring, Zara's reaction to the latest news was depressingly predictable: outrage, disgust and threats of thunderbolts. She refused to believe the fiasco of the missing charms was down to bad luck rather than Fran's incompetence, and when told about the lead on Stuart was, if anything, even more morose. 'You know what the Unicorn Lounge is, don't you? It's that new members-only club in Soho where all the fashionistas hang out. Anyone who's hired it for their wedding reception won't just be loaded: they'll be cutting-edge and uber-successful and seriously cool. Everything you're not, in fact.'

'I wouldn't be so sure of that,' Fran retorted. Ignoring Zara's disbelieving snort, she rooted around in the mess under her bed until she found a dusty bundle of magazine cuttings. 'Maybe some of this will look familiar,' she told Zara, pointing to – among others – a photo of a girl with a mane of chestnut hair, a close up of another model with a peachy-perfect face and ample bosom, and a mascara advert showing a disembodied pair of violet eyes. Zara was not impressed.

'OK, so you're hoarding pictures of half-naked models under your bed. Either it's just a phase you're going through or Ash should be worried . . . unless it's his collection, of course.'

Fran counted up to ten, then tried again. 'Remember a girl called Sabrina?'

'Sabrina as in that writer babe who seduced Quinn in the pub and gatecrashed Francesca's parents' cocktail party? Sabrina the twenty-some-thing-bimbo-bitch with the fake boobs and creepy purple eyes?'

Fran smiled.

'Omigod. Wait a minute – are you – are those – is that – did –?'

Fran smiled some more.

'That is the *sickest* thing I have ever heard,' Zara declared, torn between being outraged or admiring. 'I can't *believe* you got your boyfriend to turn you into some bionic woman made up from magazine adverts.'

'It was a social experiment,' said Fran with dignity, 'on the psychology of beauty and the cultural subjugation of the female form. And anyway, Ash wasn't my boyfriend at the time.'

'Jeez,' said Zara, shaking her head. 'So this is your brilliant plan: you get me to turn you into Sabrina again so that you can gatecrash the wedding party and schmooze Uncle Stu?'

'Do you have any better ideas?'

The genie opened her mouth and thought better of it, floated a metre or two into the air, stretched out over Fran's bed and thought some more. And some more. Then, finally: 'Nope. Bionic woman it is.'

One thing Zara was absolutely determined on: she was going to be let out of the ring to accompany Fran to the reception. 'Fact is, if you're left to your own devices, you'll just screw everything up. Again.'

'I didn't screw things up with Leila! And as for Tallulah, it's not my fault the little horror lost half the bracelet.'

'Yeah, right. And what if her uncle isn't willing to hand over the loot – how far are you prepared to go to sort it out?'

'I'll do whatever it takes.'

'Like grow a spine?' Fran started to protest, but Zara changed tack. 'Look, I know you're going to be morphed into Ms Uber-vamp, but at heart you'll still be a schoolkid of a particularly clueless kind.' She leaned back in the air and blew a plume of smoke towards the ceiling. 'If you're going to hobnob with the glitterati, you'll need back-up.'

'Let me guess: someone with street cred, backbone and effortless cool.'

'Exactly,' Zara said, apparently oblivious to the sarcasm in Fran's voice.

Making the transformation in the privacy of her own bedroom wasn't an option – there was no way Fran would be able to sneak out of the house undetected, and the idea of her nearest and dearest coming face to face with Sabrina the Plastic-boobed Bodysnatcher didn't bear thinking about. Instead, she planned to make the change in the toilets at the local shopping centre, before travelling into the

West End. But getting away from Milson Road was not quite so simple, even with a cover story to hand. Her parents (correctly) assumed that there was something that Fran wasn't telling them. She had, they both agreed, been acting very strangely – so nervous and secretive! She seemed unable to explain why her boyfriend had gone away or when he was expected back from wherever he'd gone to. Why was she spending so much time locked in her bedroom? Why did her clothes smell of cigarette smoke? And what *was* that whole business with the cat about? Fran managed to make her escape before the interrogation really got going, but she knew it was only a matter of time before she had to start coming up with some plausible answers.

At least the wish went according to plan. She wouldn't have been entirely surprised if Zara put Sabrina's ears on backwards or added a third arm, just for fun, but all things considered, the transformation was remarkably straightforward – despite the genie's initial attempt to kit out Sabrina in a red PVC catsuit plus whip.

But when the last of the prickling sensation had gone, and Fran was dusting the final trace of purple smoke from Sabrina's little black dress, even Zara seemed slightly subdued by the vision of perfection before them. For a while they both silently stared into the mirror, taking in the luscious pout, the lustrous violet eyes, the glossy tumble of chestnut hair.

'Ash must've been well gutted when seven hours of *this* was up,' said Zara at last.

'She's not his type,' Fran retorted in Sabrina's husky purr. She ran unfamiliar fingers through unfamiliar hair, feeling slightly shaky. She had never dreamed she'd be staring out of these violet eyes again. And yet she felt the stirrings of an undeniable thrill . . . A couple of teenage girls barged into the toilet. 'Do you mind?' she snapped, as one of them jostled her on the way to the sink. The girl, a big, tough-looking bottle blonde, muttered a brief apology. Ordinary Fran would never have dared to say anything. Ordinary Fran wouldn't have got away with it.

Both she and Zara set off for the reception feeling reinvigorated. Zara had even recovered her sense of humour about the situation – or rather, Ash and Fran's situation. 'Some might say it's a smart move,' she observed, 'trading your boyfriend in for a bit of antique bling. I mean, it's not like you two can be getting up to anything fun in his current state.' She flung back her head and started bawling out 'I Can't Get No *Cat*isfaction' at the top of her lungs – until a kid with a bicycle charged right through her and out the other side.

Though Fran had seen the same thing happen to Ash, she yelped nearly as loudly as Zara did. From the Commander of the Ring's perspective, the genie was so solidly flesh and blood it was hard to remember that to the rest of the world she was as insubstantial as air. Conversely, Ash had described other people as seeming slightly less defined, less real somehow, when he was looking at them through genie eyes. Perhaps this was why, after the initial shock, Zara seemed unfazed by the experience. At any rate, she was determined to make the most of being out and invisible: giving the finger to oblivious passers-by or commenting rudely on their appearance, and turning mid-air cartwheels with a flash of leopard-print thong. Though her bad mood returned when they got off the bus near a private gym and Fran vetoed a sightseeing trip to the men's locker room.

'What's the point of being invisible if I can't take advantage of the perks?' Zara complained.

'We're on a mission,' Fran said shortly. 'So no detours or distractions. Got it?'

'It's not like I have a choice,' Zara replied bitterly. 'I can't move more than seven paces away from that damned ring. And every time I get the urge to make a run for it or give you a slap or do anything fun, this stops me.' She tapped the metal band that encircled her upper left arm. 'Shooting pains if I even so much as *think* about thunderbolts.'

Maybe Fran had something to be grateful to Leila for after all.

Knowing how much depended on this afternoon, and so little about schmoozing with fashionistas, Fran should have approached the Unicorn Lounge all aquiver with nerves. Luckily, Sabrina's stomach seemed resistant to butterflies.

Naturally, her name wasn't on the invitation list but Fran was hoping Sabrina's charms would work their magic. As she approached the knot of guests waiting to enter the party, she set her sights on the least intimidating male in the line and, with a flick of her chestnut mane, swept him up in an air kiss before the poor guy knew what hit him. *Mwah Mwah.* 'Well hellooo, stranger,' Sabrina cooed, 'I didn't know *you* were going to be here. I can't *believe* it's been so long!'

The bloke looked nonplussed but, not one to look a gift horse in the mouth, obviously decided against the 'Do I know you?' line. Neither her new pal nor the doorman seemed to notice that when he gave his name to check against the list Sabrina didn't follow suit. The moment she was through the door, and just before he could start asking awkward questions, she was ready to make her getaway. 'Just off to powder my nose! Catch up later, OK?' she said brightly before shimmying off.

'Nicely done,' said Zara approvingly, then momentarily flickered out of visibility as somebody walked through her. Even in a crowded room, this didn't happen as often as one might think, almost as if the genie was giving off some kind of force field which people unconsciously responded to.

Fran headed for a corner where she could survey the scene without getting in anyone's way. The main reception room had walls painted in blood-red and purple stripes and a 1960s-style cocktail bar at one end. It was lit by black chandeliers and had a life-size unicorn's head – complete with glittery fibreglass horn – leering above the mantelpiece. Personally, Fran thought it was kind of tacky, especially for a wedding reception, but then what did she know?

'Can you see Stuart anywhere?' she asked Zara. 'Tall thin bloke with a goatee? Think he's wearing black . . .'

'Check out the pecs on that waiter!' Zara was also looking around, but showing more interest in passing eye candy than AWOL magic talismans. 'Hey, I'm guessing if it's a wedding reception there's going to be a free bar. How about a drink?'

'Like I said, we're on a mission—'

'Relax. He'll turn up sooner or later. And come face-to-face with Bionic Babe. He won't stand a chance.'

'Even so . . .'

Zara tossed her spiky head. 'Look, *Frabina*, this has all the makings of a seriously good party. The kind of party you'll never get within sniffing distance of in your normal dorky existence. So seeing as we've gone to so much trouble to get here, let's make the most of it and treat ourselves to a little R & R.'

'Fine. Just don't forget you're only here at my invitation.' Now that she had rediscovered the confidence that Sabrina inspired, there wasn't so much reason to have Zara around for back-up.

All the same, Fran was glad of the company; perhaps because Sabrina and her couldn't-give-a-stuff attitude had more in common with Zara than Fran did. Fran had been worried about being caught talking to her invisible sidekick, but as Sabrina, she found it simply wasn't an issue. Let them stare.

She shimmied over to the bar. 'Hi there, I'll have two orange –' she caught Zara's eye – 'Two glasses of champagne, please.'

'Attagirl.' Zara downed hers in one, smacking her lips in relish. As soon as she had the drink in her hand it vanished from ordinary sight, returning to view when she placed the empty flute on the counter. The barman did a double take, blinked, and went to take another order. He could've sworn that gorgeous model-type had been talking to herself a minute ago, but when he looked at her again, her gaze was so steady, her expression so chilly, he decided he must have imagined it.

Fran finished off her own drink pretty quickly too. She decided Zara was right: she'd been through hell the last twenty-four hours – surely she deserved a break? Things would be a lot less stressful if she relaxed a bit. That's what Ash used to tell her when he was her genie, anyway. But Fran didn't want to think about Ash just now. It was too painful. Instead, she tossed back her chestnut locks, moistened her glossy lips and headed off to look for Stuart.

The party was filling up; in fact, the air was positively vibrating with the sound of air-kisses. Fran had only been to one wedding reception, when she was quite a bit younger, and her abiding impression was of lots of old ladies in big hats, the bride in white ruffles and whining kids with cake in their hair. But there were no little kids or old ladies here and there wasn't a white ruffle in sight – the bride, she decided, must be the girl in the silver-and-pearl cocktail dress, posing for photos under the unicorn. Most of the female guests were expensive-looking blondes wearing the kind of outfit that reminded Fran of Leila on their second meeting: lots of jangling jewellery and layers of exotic prints. Their male counterparts tended towards scruffy retro haircuts and sharp, non-scruffy retro suits.

It took her a while to find Stuart as there were two other rooms to look through as well as the one with the bar. Zara wasn't much help – she was too busy helping herself to passing trays of drinks and nibbles. (Her favourite trick was to suck up a person's drink using a straw, or else to drop bits of canapé into female guests' handbags/hair/cleavages.) Finally, Fran spotted her quarry talking to an older bloke by one of the windows. She accepted another glass of champagne from a passing waiter, then sidled over to plot her next move.

Close up, Stuart didn't look any more approachable than she remembered; although he wasn't bad-looking exactly, he had the same petulant expression as his niece. Fran couldn't see any sign of the miniature ring, but she didn't think there was much danger he'd got rid of it en route from Talullah's house to the reception. There was something eerily compelling about those charms.

So far, the conversation seemed to be one long whinge about how weddings make women extra neurotic. Stuart was particularly bitter on the subject, since his girlfriend had been giving him a hard time for forgetting their one-year anniversary.

'I mean, you want your woman to be a little insecure, don't you? But I tell you what, Lily's emotional needs are turning out to be seriously high maintenance: whining on about how she hardly ever sees me, how I never give her compliments – so I asked her who's fault that was, what with the weight she's put on?' Both men sniggered furtively. 'Anyway, I cobbled some anniversary trinket together at the last minute, gave her the whole spiel about planning it for ages, wanting it to be a surprise, blah blah blah. So I'm back in her good books for now.'

Stuart's mate laughed and said something about apron strings. Meanwhile, Fran's ears had pricked up at the mention of the last-minute present. Stuart was obviously a total loser, so ten to one he was probably a total cheapskate as well. The kind of loser cheapskate who'd pass off a broken-off freebie as a romantic gift, in fact . . . Trouble was, it would have been a lot easier to charm the charm off Stuart than to prise it away from his girlfriend.

Zara reappeared at her elbow. 'You made contact yet?'

'Not yet. But I reckon I know what's happened to our missing talisman.'

'I'm sorry, did you say something?' Stuart's friend had gone to the bar and he and Sabrina were now on their own. 'I don't think we've met. I'm Stuart,' he said, offering his hand.

'Sabrina,' said Fran, sighing inwardly. His hand held on to hers for more time than was strictly necessary and his eyes were fixed firmly on Sabrina's cleavage.

'A friend of the bride's?'

'Er, that's right.'

'Lucky her. You look like a girl who knows how to have fun.'

The genie gave a snort and helped herself to the olive from his martini. 'What I don't get,' she said conversationally, 'is how minging loser men always think they have a chance with hot babes. I mean, minging loser girls don't go chatting up hot guys. They just drool from a distance.'

Fran smirked. 'I guess insecure guys are still more confident than insecure girls.'

'Or more desperate,' put in Zara.

'Interesting point,' said Stuart, even though Fran's out-of-context remark didn't make any sort of sense. He gave a gallant leer. 'Though I'm sure with looks like yours, you've never had an insecure moment in your life.'

'Insecure like your girlfriend, you mean?' she asked.

'Girlfriend? What – oh, you mean Lily! Ha ha. So you heard that little joke I had with Simon did you? Er . . . Lily and I have a very informal relationship. Open, you might say,' he added hopefully.

Fran and Zara exchanged looks. 'Yeah – open like a sewer,' observed the genie.

'And where is Lily now?'

'Who knows? But to get back to you—'

'What does she look like?'

Stuart was distinctly nonplussed. 'Er, short brown hair, brown eyes, quite ordinary.'

'What's she wearing?'

'Some dress with polka dots. Nothing special. Whereas *you*—'

'Fantastic.' Sabrina flashed him a dazzling smile. 'You've been most helpful.' And she turned on her heel and walked briskly away.

Fran decided to start her search for Lily in the room with the dance floor. There were already quite a few people there, although since they were all uber-trendy types, any movement was restricted to occasional head nodding, half-closed eyes and rhythmic twitching. Fran hung around the edges, on the lookout for brown-haired, brown-eyed 'ordinary' girls, while Zara went to persecute the DJ by reshuffling his carefully organised pile of records whenever his back was turned.

'Bride or groom?'

Fran turned, mentally steeling herself for another leering Stuart-type, only to find she was face to face with Sabrina's male equivalent: tall, manly and chiselled, with tousled fair hair and ice-green eyes. She gulped. 'Bride. We're old friends,' she said. Then, recklessly, 'Practically since the cradle!'

The green eyes twinkled. 'Well, in that case, I'm sure she won't mind if I do a bit of cradle-snatching.'

Before she could protest, he had taken her hands in his and pulled her into the middle of the dancers. Fran had a moment of blind panic – she didn't know where to start when it came to rhythmic twitching – before remembering that she was Sabrina, and Sabrina could make *anything* look good. Ash had been teaching her some ancient Baghdad-style dance moves, and though she'd been sceptical at first they'd had a lot of fun doing some practice wriggling and giggling. Now she tried an experimental hip-shake followed by a bottom-wiggle and one of those snaky arm-waves Ash liked, and found the moves fitted surprisingly well into the R & B track that was playing. She got some slightly startled looks, but the guy she was dancing with didn't seem to mind. In fact, after that, quite a lot of people seemed to want to dance with her. She shimmied from one partner to another, until she had got through quite a number.

'Didn't know you had it in you, Roper!' Zara

cackled in her ear. 'Do you realize you're getting death stares from every other girl in the room?'

'They're just jealous,' she retorted, running manicured fingers through Sabrina's lustrous hair.

'That's the spirit. You're a lot more fun like this – Sabrina must bring out the best in you.' The next moment she had cut in to bump and grind alongside Fran's latest dance partner, who, perhaps aware of her presence on some subconscious level, moved back to allow space for her gyrations. 'You know, she doesn't look half so hot in real life,' she told him, leaning in to nibble on his ear.

Fran barely noticed. Zara's little comment had brought her up short. Ash had never thought Sabrina brought out the best in her; in fact, despite his admittedly shallow streak, Ash had been anti-Sabrina from the start. What would he think if he could see her now, dancing away as if she didn't have a care in the world, when the course of the rest of his life was at stake?

Frowning to herself, she shouldered her way out of the crowd. It was only when she reached the edge of the dance floor that she realized her mobile was going off.

It was her mum.

She didn't answer the phone, of course. How could she? There was no way Mrs Roper would be fooled into thinking Sabrina's husky purr was her daughter's voice. But after the call went to voicemail, she saw that this was the third time her mum had tried to phone her in the last twenty minutes. She had a missed call from Amira too. Uh-oh.

* * * * ★ 77 ★ * * * *

Fran set off to find somewhere to listen to her messages, the pull of the ring dragging Zara in her wake. Since the bathroom was heaving with gossiping girls reapplying lipgloss, the best she could do was nip outside and take shelter behind a nearby skip. It was bad news. Granny Roper had had 'a funny turn' and Mrs Roper was taking her to be checked out at the hospital; her dad was currently stuck in traffic on the way there from his Saturday footy game. Mrs Larkin, a neighbour, was looking after Mickey and Beth, but she had an appointment at half-three – could Fran go home in time to take over?

The second message was from Amira, who Mrs Roper had also phoned in her attempt to reach Fran. She said she'd made up some story about Fran popping out to the shops and leaving her mobile behind, but this excuse wouldn't wash for much longer. The third and fourth messages were also from Mrs Roper, and increasingly frantic in tone.

Fran swore. She'd made the wish at about half eleven and had several hours of Sabrina left to go. 'My parents might not be back for *ages*,' she wailed. 'Even if they do make other arrangements for the kids, Amira can't keep covering for me. What are they going to think if I take off for the afternoon, when my little brother and sister are home alone and my granny's in hospital?'

'Hmm. That you're an irresponsible, untrustworthy cow, I would say.'

'But there must be some way we can use the ring's magic . . . maybe if I wish I could go back to being me for the rest of the afternoon—'

'No way! We're on a mission, *remember*? No detours or distractions, *remember*? You can't leave now, not when you're within grabbing distance of the charm!'

Fran groaned and put Sabrina's head in her hands. It didn't help that she was beginning to feel the effects of alcohol on an empty stomach that had been jiggling vigorously around a dance floor. Too many crises had taken place for her to think clearly about this latest one, or what her immediate priority should be. If only she could split herself into two . . .

At this thought, a wild idea came into her head. In retrospect, it was not a very good one, but ever since Leila had appeared, Fran had only just been keeping hysteria at bay. 'I've got it! It's simple – I'll use a wish to turn you into me! That way *you* can go back to Milson Road and look after Mickey and Beth. *You* can be the dutiful daughter while I set about getting the charm back from Stuart!'

'Eurgh! No *way*! That's *disgusting*. Like something out a particularly sick horror film.' Zara made a violent retching sound. 'Why would I want to be imprisoned in your lumpish body while you get to vamp it up as Ms Plastic Fantastic here? I mean, *euwwww* . . . And to get back to my original point, I still don't see why we should waste a wish just to make your domestic life easier.'

'This is really important,' she pleaded. 'It's an emergency. *Please*.'

A calculating gleam came into Zara's eye. 'All right then,' she said slowly. 'I'll do it. But on one condition – that you promise to use one of your remaining wishes on something that *I* want. Something personal, of my choosing.'

'But that's the whole point of the wishes! To return you and Ash to human form. Isn't that what you want more than anything else?'

'Course. But with a bit of luck, and as long as you don't keep messing everything up, we should have a wish or two going spare. And if we do, I want to stake my claim to it.' Zara smiled nastily. 'You know, it's a big responsibility, pretending to be someone else for an afternoon. Especially when that someone else is so dissimilar to me in every way . . . I mean, you wouldn't want me to disgrace your, would you?'

Good point: there was no reason to force the genie to make a wish that she could then go on to sabotage. Fran winced as the wooziness in her head temporarily cleared to reveal a multitude of unpleasant possibilities. She and Zara eyed each other warily. 'So if I agree to let you use a spare wish, you promise to fulfil this one without setting out to cause trouble?'

'That's the deal.'

'Then I'll take it . . . and so I wish,' she said quickly, before she could think better of it, 'that for the remainder of my time as Sabrina, Zara would appear in human form as me, Fran Roper.'

Over the course of her entanglement with the ring, Fran had seen – and done – some very peculiar things. Nothing, however, compared to the strangeness of looking at herself through Sabrina's eyes.

She braced herself for Zara to burst into hysterics or abuse of some description, but in fact Zara was as dumbstruck as she was. More so, even. For a while they just stood there, blinking at each other.

'This is the – the most – I don't – I'm not –' stuttered Zara before grinding to a halt. She stared at Fran's small, soft hands, still bearing traces of glittery varnish around the nails, then put one hand tremulously up to her – Fran's – long pale hair. She gulped. 'Gotta tell you, I'm feeling pretty freaked out right now.'

'Me too,' whispered Fran. A naturally shy person, she found it hard enough listening to herself on a voicemail recording or the demo tapes of the Butterflies that Amira had made. But to hear her voice – to *see* her voice – coming out of a mirror image turned flesh and blood . . . Did she *really* sound, move, look like that? Everything about the person she was looking at was one hundred per cent familiar to her, and yet utterly strange.

Zara was trying out Fran's facial expressions. On Fran's face, her trademark sneer translated as a rather comical grimace. 'Right then,' she said, a little less certainly than usual, 'let's get this freak show on the road. You've got a curse to undo and I've got a couple of babies to sit.'

'Oh. Yes. Of course.' Fran was still light-headed with shock. Although she knew there were lots of things she should instruct/warn/advise Zara about, for the moment she couldn't think of how or where to start. 'Um . . . What you need to do first, I think, is phone my mum to say sorry, you've only just got her messages and that you're on your way. Best to keep it brief. Then go back to Milson Road and wait with Mickey and Beth until my parents get back. Try to say or do as little as possible, really.'

'Suits me.'

'You remember our deal?'

'I'm in possession of your plus-sized body, not your pea-sized brain, thank you very much. Yes, I remember the deal – seeing as we made it all of two minutes ago.' Zara gave a most un-Fran-like snort, and Fran's misgivings increased sharply. She put them to one side – it wasn't as if she had much choice – and pressed on.

'Here're my keys and mobile. I'll use yours.' They had agreed that she should carry Zara's phone so that she could text replies to messages from Zara's friends and family, keeping up the pretence that everything was normal. Fran was glad of it now. 'Call me if there are any problems.'

There was another awkward pause. Fran couldn't stop staring at herself-who-wasn't – she'd always wondered what it would be like to have an identical twin, but this was different. Madly different.

'OK.' Abruptly, Zara gave herself a shake and turned to go, her initial movements a little unsteady as she accustomed herself to somebody else's stride. It had been the same when Fran first morphed into Sabrina.

'Look after me – I mean yourself,' Fran said with a tremor in her voice.

Zara gave her the finger in reply.

Fran went back to the party with a heavy heart. She was already regretting her hasty wish but at the same time she still didn't see what else she could have done. A little voice warned that having an evil twin on the loose was hardly a guarantee for an easy life, but Fran clung to the fact that it was very much in Zara's interest to behave. Anyway, it was too late now.

Before returning to the Lily-quest, she spent a few moments skulking against a wall in the main room, trying to collect her thoughts and steel her nerve for the task at hand. She wished strongly that Ash was here, even in cat form, to stop her feeling sorry for herself, and heaved a mournful sigh at the exact same time as the guy standing next to her. They caught each other's eye and grinned a bit shamefacedly.

'Aren't you enjoying yourself then?' he asked.

'Not really, no,' she confessed.

'Me neither. It's just not my scene, all these media and fashion-types – no offence.'

'None taken.' He did look a bit out of place in his tux, in comparison to the other fashionably dishevelled blokes with their designer suits, but she decided she liked the look of him. For one thing, he was the first male she'd encountered since she'd been in Sabrina-form who hadn't gone through the whole double-take/dropped-jaw/drooling routine. It had been fun at first, but the novelty was beginning to wear off.

'Do you know many people here?' She'd noticed that his eyes kept darting back to a girl on the other side of the room.

'I went to uni with the groom. Then there's . . . well, my ex-girlfriend.' He sighed again. 'Sadly, I'm not sure that counts.'

'You miss her?'

'Like you wouldn't believe.'

'I miss my boyfriend,' Fran said abruptly.

'Yeah?' He looked at her, not with lust or admiration, but straightforward friendliness. Like she was ordinary. She had a sudden urge to confide everything, though she knew if she did he'd be calling for the men in white coats.

'We're in a kind of complicated situation.' *Like you wouldn't believe . . .*

'Well, whatever it is, you make sure you sort it out. Because before you know it, it's too late.'

She smiled with new determination. 'I won't let that happen.'

'Good luck.' He was looking over at the girl again. A girl, Fran noticed, in a polka-dot dress and wearing some kind of pendant around her neck.

Zara had set off for Milson Road more or less intending to stick to her side of the deal, subject to a few minor adjustments. Being confined to Fran's totally inferior body was a bummer of course, but that didn't mean she couldn't make the most of things, did it?

As soon as she was out of Fran's view, Zara peeled off her jumper to reveal a black cotton vest, which she pulled as indecently low as she could manage while hoiking up her bra straps for dramatic effect. Then she undid Fran's plait and wildly tousled her hair, bundling half of it up in a messy high ponytail and leaving the other half to hang in wavy strands around her face. Finally, she sauntered into a chemist's to swipe some blood-red lipstick, silver hair glitter and black eyeliner, which she applied thickly in a cat's-eye effect.

Zara was busy admiring Fran's new, improved reflection in a shop window when her mobile began to beep abruptly. Hell! She'd forgotten all about her promise to call Fran's mum first thing. Never mind, Mrs Roper was bound to be as much of a pushover as her daughter was –

'Fran! About time! Why the hell haven't you been answering your phone?' squawked the indignant voice on the other end of the line.

'Why, hello there, Mother,' said Zara in supersweet tones, 'how delightful to hear from you.'

'Where are you? Why aren't you home yet? Why haven't you *called*? Mrs Larkin is waiting outside with the kids *right now*—'

'Fret not, Mother dearest, I'm almost there.' Zara soothed. She didn't really believe Fran spoke to her parents like someone out of a Jane Austen novel, but if she had to play the good girl, she might as well do it properly.

'What on earth's got into you?' asked Mrs Roper in exasperation. 'Listen, the good news is that Gran's feeling better, though they're keeping her in for a few hours for observation. Dad's arrived, so I'll be able to leave before too long. In the meantime, make sure—'

'Frightfully sorry, old girl, but you're breaking up.' Zara made buzzing sounds into the mouthpiece. 'Don't vex yourself though. Everything's under control.'

She was indeed already turning the corner into Milson Road and could see Mickey and Beth waiting on the doorstep of Number 35, accompanied by an anxious-looking mumsy type. Mrs Larkin, presumably.

'Afternoon all,' she purred, before giving the finger to a passing car which had honked appreciatively at the sight of low top, lipstick and swagger. 'Sorry for the delay. Technical hitch and all that jazz.'

Mrs Larkin's welcoming smile was slightly uncertain. 'Hello there, Fran. Is there any news on your poor granny?'

'Doesn't look like she'll be popping her clogs just yet. You know what these old fogeys are like though. Mostly they're just after a bit of attention.'

Mrs Larkin's smile was now distinctly forced. 'And . . . er . . . how's that nice boyfriend of yours?'

'Ash? Oh, he's an *animal* . . . which is just the way I like it, if you know what I mean,' she added with a wink and a smirk.

'Bad girl!' said Beth suddenly. 'Me wants Fan Fan! Go 'way, bad girl!'

Mrs Larkin shot her a worried look. 'Are you sure you'll be all right looking after the little ones?'

'It's babysitting, not brain surgery, lady. Anyway, shouldn't you be off? I thought you had an appointment at the local cake bake or whatever desperate housewifely stuff it is you do.'

'Well, *really* –'

But Zara didn't bother to wait for a reply, being preoccupied with opening the door and hustling the Roper kids through it. Once inside, they stood huddled together at the bottom of the stairs and regarded her solemnly. Actually, it was kind of creepy. The little one had this weird unblinking stare and the big one, Mike or Mick or whatever his name was, looked to be an even bigger geek than his older sister.

'Why are you wearing all that make-up?' he said at last.

'Cos I was tired of being a frumpy loser.'

'It's kind of cool . . . Fran, what did you mean when you said Ash was an animal?'

'Who can say?' Zara tapped the side of her nose in a mysterious manner. 'Let me tell you, bro, there's a lot you don't know about that Arabian hottie of mine.'

'Bad girl!' Beth piped up again.

'Shut it, blondie.' Even when softened by Fran's features, the ferocity of Zara's glare reduced Beth to a wobbly lipped silence. 'Now, do I need to, like, do anything with you kids?'

'Like what?'

'Feed you pills, put you to bed, wipe your noses . . . I dunno, babysitting things.'

'Well,' said Mickey, furrowing his brow in bewilderment, 'I was just going to go play in my room and watch TV.'

'Sounds good to me. You can take the little one – what's-her-face – with you. And if you want to play with matches or anything, just check with me first, OK?'

Zara watched them go with satisfaction. Honestly, she didn't know what Fran was so stressed about. This impersonation thing was a cinch. Feeling super-virtuous, she got out Fran's phone and texted her own mobile: KIDS SORTED NO WORRIES.

Duties done, she wandered into the Roper's kitchen and had a rummage through the fridge. Ooh yum . . . lemon cheesecake. Best of all, she could eat as much as she liked and every calorie would end up on Fran's thighs! At the thought of Fran/Sabrina necking champagne with the glitterati, she decided to help herself to one of Mr Roper's beers as well. And she might as well have a fag while she was at it . . . OK, so this wasn't strictly what Fran would consider 'good behaviour', but Zara felt she had conducted herself in an exemplary fashion so far. And hell, she deserved a break.

She tuned the radio to a gangster-rap station, turned the volume up loud, and settled down to drink her beer, smoke her fag and work her way through the cheesecake. Mmmmmmm.

Mrs Roper did not react well to finding her eldest daughter lounging half-undressed with her feet on the table, fag in one hand, beer in the other, looking – as she said later – like a refugee from the *Jerry Springer Show*. In fact, she let out a shriek and nearly dropped the bag of groceries she was carrying.

In fairness, Zara did actually feel quite guilty. She'd meant to dispose of at least some of the evidence before the rest of the family arrived. Now that she'd been caught, however, she decided she'd have to face it out.

'Good afternoon, Mother dear, what a lovely surprise. I, um, didn't know you'd be back so soon.'

'So I can see,' said Mrs Roper tartly.

'Yeah, but I can explain. Er . . . fact is, I'm . . . I'm in the middle of a personal crisis.'

* * * * * ★ 88 ★ * * * * *

'Since when?'

Zara fixed her eyes on Fran's mother reproachfully. 'Since I realized the randomness of life in a godless universe –' she thought for a bit – 'and that I'll never fit into size-ten clothes.'

Mrs Roper was looking uncertain now. 'Well, I can see you're upset—'

'Upset? I'm, like, in emotional meltdown!'

'All I'm saying, love, is that this sort of behaviour is only going to make you feel worse. I don't know exactly what's going on with you and Ash, but I'm not at all sure he's a good influence on you.'

But at this point Zara lost patience. 'Jesus! I'm *fifteen*. I realize that up till now the wildest thing Fr – I have ever done is not recycle my organic yogurt pots or whatever, but cut me some slack, OK?'

'You're usually so responsible—'

'Responsible? Repressed, you mean. At least Ash has livened me up a bit, I'll say that for him. Or do you actually want me to spend the best years of my life as a forty-something frump trapped in a teenage body?'

It was probably just as well that Mickey chose this moment to burst into the kitchen. 'Fran,' he said, 'there's a boy outside who wants to speak to you.'

Zara was already halfway out the door. 'On second thoughts,' she called cheerily over her shoulder, 'I can guarantee this is probably the shortest-lived teenage rebellion in history.'

She found Quinn waiting on the doorstep. 'Boy, am I glad to see you,' she purred, pulling down

Fran's vest by another notch or two and moistening Fran's blood-red lips.

Quinn looked almost as gobsmacked as Mrs Roper had been. 'Uh, hi, Fran. You're looking . . . different.'

'I thought it was time for a change of image.'

Quinn gave the new image further consideration. On balance, he liked what he saw, and he was about to say so – before remembering he was supposed to be the new, improved Quinn, who was only interested in Fran for her warm heart and sympathetic ear. He hastily rearranged his face into a soulful expression.

'Anyway, I was wondering if you'd maybe like to hang out for a while. So we could . . . you know . . . talk things over.'

'Try and stop me,' said Zara. Mrs Roper was still squawking in the hall and she shut the door behind them hastily. 'Got a lighter on you?'

Elsewhere, the real Fran and fake Sabrina were making progress. After her encounter with the Sighing Bloke, she'd gone after the polka-dot girl and tracked her down in the loos, where she was chatting with two other girls by the basin. 'I was so sure he'd forgotten,' she was saying, 'when all the time he was waiting for it to arrive from the antique dealer's. Who said romance is dead?'

'It's gorgeous. So tiny and yet so ornate!' cooed the first girl.

'And a *ring*, no less,' put in the other girl, with a significant smile. 'That's a pretty big hint, if you ask me.'

'Yes,' said the first girl flicking her hair. 'Better not let poor old Tim see it. He's already moping around like a wet weekend.'

'Tim's here? No *way*,' said the second. 'Talk about blast from the past! It's like he totally dropped off the map after you guys broke up. Right, Lil?'

But at this Lily looked troubled and stopped playing with the little charm.

'Uh, could I see it?' Fran intervened.

The other girls looked up in surprise, followed by the suspicion Sabrina usually aroused in her fellow females. Lily, however, shrugged and passed it over.

Dangling on a silver chain was a thumbnail-sized version of the ring that hung around Fran's neck and was currently tucked into Sabrina's pocket. It even had a tiny purple gem. Her hands trembled with longing. Should she just make a dash for it? She was pretty sure that's what Zara would say if she was here now. Fran didn't want to cause trouble for Lily, who seemed too nice for the likes of Stuart, but two people's futures were at stake, not to mention her own happiness. And if she didn't act soon she'd miss her chance –

Lily put her hand out for the charm, her smile looking slightly fixed as Fran's hands clenched over her prize. Too late. And even if she did try and make a run for it, she wouldn't get very far. Not with these heels, and not with the dagger stares Lily's friends were giving her.

Inwardly cursing her lack of nerve, Fran uncurled her clammy fingers and let Lily pick up the chain. Then she stumbled out the door. What an idiot. Frankly, she didn't see how she could have handled the situation any worse. If only she'd had Zara's gutsiness: snatched the charm, pushed Lily to the floor and made a run for it. Or had Ash with her, with his gift of the gab. He'd have concocted some effortlessly plausible story and got Lily to pass it over on a silver plate . . .

OK, time to find a Plan B. Maybe she could get Lily on her own once she was back to Fran the fresh-faced schoolgirl, and explain that there's been some kind of mix-up and that the ring was in fact hers? Or would it be easier for Sabrina to schmooze Stuart and get him to do her dirty work instead?

'Hey there, gorgeous. I thought I'd lost you.'

It looked like her decision had been made.

'And now we've found each other again.' Fran somehow managed to smile, then flutter Sabrina's eyelashes suggestively. She didn't like the idea of going behind Lily's back any more than the idea of taking the charm by force, but she was running out of options. 'I was, um, hoping I'd bump into you.'

'You were?'

'Absolutely. You see, I've fallen in love with your friend Lily –' Sabrina fixed him with huge violet eyes – 'with your friend Lily's new pendant.'

Stuart blinked. No doubt about it, the girl was seriously odd. Or rather, *enigmatic*, he corrected himself. Strange ugly people were odd, strange beautiful people were 'mysterious' and 'individual'.

'Such a lovely gesture,' she was crooning. 'The kind of gift I've been longing for my whole life . . .'

'I'm full of lovely gestures,' Stuart crooned in

return. He slipped his arm around her waist. 'Why don't we sit down and I can tell you *all* about them.'

'And the ring,' she reminded him forcing herself not to shudder. Or smack him in the eye. 'Lily's ring.'

'Lily who?' he murmured as he began to pull her towards a darkened alcove.

'As in Lily your girlfriend of one year,' came an outraged voice behind them.

It was the girl in question of course, standing alongside one of her friends from the loos. Stuart shoved Fran away so abruptly that she nearly fell into the buffet table.

'Lil! Thank goodness you're here! This woman just won't take no for an answer.'

'Didn't exactly look as if you were fighting her off,' Lily retorted.

'Hang on – that's the girl who was all over your pendant!' exclaimed her friend.

'Yes, you're right!' said Stuart eagerly. 'The ring! That's all she's been going on about. She's probably a jewel thief, one of those international con-artists. She saw the value of an antique piece and—'

Fran snorted. 'Garbage. You only got it cos it snapped off your niece's tacky goth charm bracelet.'

'How do you know – oh my God, you've been stalking me! See!' He turned to Lily in appeal. 'She's a bunny boiler. A psycho. You can't believe a word she says.'

But Lily was looking at him through narrowed eyes. 'I thought you said the charm came from an antique jeweller's in Paris?'

'Sweetie, I promise you—'

'There she is!' Two other girls had marched up. 'That's the bimbo who was putting the moves on Christian!'

'Who's Christian?' asked Fran in bewilderment.

'My fiancé,' replied the other new arrival with a glare. 'Tall, blond, handsome? The one everybody saw you slow-dancing with.'

'Him and every other man at this party!'

'So is this girl a guest or a gatecrasher?' demanded Lily.

'She's a con-artist, I tell you! A bunny-boiling jewel thief!'

'Sleazy little slapper!'

'Can't get her own man so she has to go after everyone else's!'

'For God's sake,' Fran said in exasperation, 'it's not my fault all the males at this party are lying scumbuckets –'

At this, Christian's fiancée slapped her across the face. It was absolutely the last straw. Fran threw a glass of champagne over her dress. Her sidekick screeched, grabbed a cream-filled meringue from the table and flung it into Sabrina's hair. Fran dumped a bowl of strawberries over Stuart. So did Lily. That was when security was called.

In some ways, things were going better than Quinn had ever expected, but in other ways . . . Well, it was hard work trying to read Fran in this new and surprising mood. As the two of them sauntered along the road, he was finding that all his carefully rehearsed conversation openers were making little headway. He'd made a tentative remark about 'the

* * * * * ★ 94 ★ * * * * *

new me', only for Fran to snort dismissively and say, 'Hell yes, when's the old one coming back?'

'But I'm trying to make a new identity for myself. As a better person. I thought that's what you—'

'Oh, sure. I mean, it's true Fr – I only go for pure-hearted guys,' Fran had said hastily. 'Because I'm so sweet and innocent and everything. But that doesn't mean you have to turn into a total loser, does it? Not when,' she added with a suggestive smile, 'we could be having *real* fun.'

Equally mystifying was the business with Amira. Just as he and Fran reached the end of Milson Road, Quinn was dismayed to see his ex-girlfriend charge round the corner, rush up to Fran and pull her into a bear hug.

'Fran! I've been worried about you, babe! Have you managed to sort whatever you had to sort out? Are you OK? Did you get into trouble with your mum?'

For some reason, Fran did not look particularly thrilled to see her friend. 'All under control,' she said brusquely.

Amira shot Quinn a confused look. 'Whatcha doing with *him*? Don't tell me he's mixed up in this mystery dilemma of yours.'

'We're just hanging out. No big deal.'

'But – but what about Ash?'

'That's not really any of your business,' Fran retorted.

Amira's bewilderment turned to indignation. 'Whoa there. *You* made it my business when you asked me to cover for you this afternoon. And when *you* skived our rehearsal to hang out with my ex. Or have you forgotten how this two-faced creep ripped off me and my music?'

'It was never meant to be a rip-off,' Quinn muttered. 'Lots of bands do cover versions of artists they, um, admire.'

Amira's eyes flashed, but when she answered him her tone was light. 'I see. Maybe I should've been flattered. Like you'd set up my very own tribute band.'

'And at least Firedog brought your work to a new audience.'

'With some artistic improvements along the way?'

Quinn looked thoughtful. 'Well, I did always think that the lyrics to *Looking-Glass Girl* worked better once the genders were reversed. *Looking-Glass Boy* just didn't—'

'On the subject of gender,' Amira said, still in the same sweet tone, 'I'd stop right there if you want to walk away with your manhood intact.' She turned to Fran. 'I didn't name us the Stamping Butterflies for nothing, girl. And right now, I feel the need for my hobnail boots coming on.'

'Don't even think about it!' Fran tossed her head. 'All that battle of the bands stuff is *so* yesterday's news. It's time to make love, not war, like the hippies said.'

Then she took Quinn by the arm and swaggered away down the street.

Sabrina hadn't been ejected from the party without a fight. The stress and frustration of the last couple of days had pushed Fran to breaking point, and when she'd finally snapped it was strangely exhilarating. Swearing, screaming, kicking, arms flailing, eyes flashing, it had taken one security guard and two burly rugby players to get rid of her. Now that the adrenalin had worn off, she was sitting slumped against the skip, meringue and strawberries mushed into Sabrina's shining hair, scratch marks and bruises marring Sabrina's peach-smooth skin, a jagged tear in Sabrina's chic little cocktail dress. But Sabrina's dress wasn't the only thing in ruins. All their plans, all their hopes . . . A whole wish wasted. She put her head on her knees and groaned aloud. How would she be able to face Zara and Ash?

'Here. I thought you might like to have this.' Fran looked up to see Lily holding out the miniature ring in the palm of her hand. She gawped in disbelief.

'Wh-wh –'

'Well, I was about to fling it back in the lying scumbucket's face, but then I thought that would be a waste. Specially as you were so keen on it.'

Fran gulped and clasped it tightly in her fist before Lily could come to her senses and change her mind. 'But aren't you mad at me?'

'Nah.' Lily sighed ruefully and sat down beside her. 'Way I see it, I kind of think you did me a favour. I guess I was kidding myself about Stuart. Trying to pretend things were OK, when I knew we were never right for each other.'

Relief surged through Fran, sweeter than the whipped cream dripping from her eyebrow. 'Bet I know someone who'll be pleased to hear that.' She grinned widely. 'See, I met this sad-looking bloke in a tux. Said he's an old friend of yours . . .'

This time it was Lily's turn to gawp. 'D'you mean T-Tim? How—'

'He couldn't take his eyes off you. There I was doing my sex-bomb thing, and he barely even noticed.'

Lily blushed. 'I find that hard to believe.'

'Well, *exactly*!' said Fran recklessly. 'Because let's face it, I'm a hundred per cent irresistible. Since I've looked like this, I've never met a bloke who hasn't fallen into lust at first sight – until your Tim came along, that is. So it *must* be love.'

They looked at each other and started to laugh.

'Well,' said Lily, half-gasping, half-giggling, 'I don't know who you are or what on earth you're playing at . . . but I'm glad we met.' She looked at the charm again. 'Actually, I never really liked it. Even though it's pretty, there's something a bit creepy about it, don't you think?'

'I know what you mean,' said Fran. 'But it has its uses.'

Fran's text message – YES! GOT RING ALL OK – caught Zara by surprise. She and Quinn were getting on so well that she'd temporarily forgotten she'd borrowed somebody else's body for the occasion. In the days when Zara had been a favoured member of Quinn's entourage, Francesca Goldsworthy, Firedog's official pin-up, had always taken the lion's share of his attention. Zara hadn't much minded; she'd always found him a bit too pretty boy for her taste, but times had changed. Unshaven, with his floppy blond locks cut short and new shadows under his eyes and cheekbones, Quinn looked a lot older. Edgier. Sexier, in fact . . .

Fran's text brought her back to reality of the situation with a jolt. She was also newly mindful of her altercations with Mrs Roper and Amira – and the inevitable fallout once Fran got wind of them. Zara decided it was time to be a little more proactive. Ash had warned her that she herself couldn't touch any part of the curse bracelet, but that didn't mean she couldn't do some research on the missing charm. It occurred to her that Fran was a lot less likely to fixate on the small print of their agreement if the genie tracked down the cat trinket on her own. And so far, Daisy Adams was their only lead.

'So, Quinn,' she said abruptly, 'what's your little sister up to these days?'

Quinn's usual approach to his sibling was 'out of sight, out of mind'. But though he hadn't realized Fran knew about his sister, it seemed like a good opportunity to come over all warm-hearted and brotherly. 'Daisy's doing great, thanks. She's a very special kid.'

'I bet she is. I *adore* small children! They're . . . so . . . small. And wholesome.' She paused. 'I'd love to meet her, you know. Is she around?'

'Dunno. Probably. She was meant to be going to some birthday party but it fell through, I think.'

Zara was about to propose they go in search of Adams Junior, when something caught her eye that put all thoughts of charm-recovery out of her mind. 'Hey – isn't that Rob and Sadie over there?'

It was indeed the Golden Couple of Conville

Secondary, sucking face in the window of a coffee shop Zara and Quinn were just passing. Zara smiled: here was the perfect opportunity to launch Phase Two of the Quinn Adams Rehabilitation Plan.

'Time for peace, love and caffeinated beverages. Let's go say hi.'

Before Quinn could protest, Zara/Fran had already marched over to the snogfest. 'Hello, Rob, hello, Sadie. What a lovely surprise.' Nobody else seemed to think so. In fact, Sadie looked confused, Rob hostile and Quinn martyred. 'I'm so glad we ran into you guys! Mind if we join you?'

'It'll be a tight squeeze,' said Rob, with a leer at Fran's cleavage.

Sadie tossed her hair. 'I'm sorry Ash isn't with you. How *is* that gorgeous boyfriend of yours?' she asked pointedly.

'Furry.'

'Huh?'

'Foreign. You know – clash of cultures and that. Come and help me get the drinks in and I'll tell you *all* about it.' Zara took Sadie by the arm and drew her towards the counter, leaving the two boys scowling across the table. Sadie was sufficiently intrigued by the Quinn-Fran development to play along, though once they joined the queue she kept casting anxious looks over her shoulder.

'I hope Robbie and Quinn will be all right. After they had that big fight—'

'Puh-lease. This stupid feud is so pointless. And boring. Don't you think it's about time things got back to how they used to be? Then everything would be cool again. You and Rob, Zara and Quinn, hanging out, making music, calling the shots . . . Best of all, this time you wouldn't have me and Francesca cramping your style.'

'That's what Zara keeps saying.'

'That's because Zara is totally right,'

Sadie frowned. 'I'm not sure. I know she's my friend and everything but I gotta say, she's been *so* not fun lately.'

'What do you mean?' Zara demanded while giving their order.

Sadie gave the adorable giggle that was her prelude to an A-grade bitching session. Zara had heard it many times but she'd never thought it could be used behind her own back. 'For one thing, she's just, like, totally obsessed with the whole Firedog breakup. Keeps coming out with all this freaky conspiracy stuff, you know?'

'No,' Zara managed to say through gritted teeth.

'Everyone has moved on. I mean, look at you. You used to be this boring mousy little thing, but now you're, like, approaching cool. Almost. Then there's me and Robbie, of course, and Robbie's new band . . . You'd think Zara would be happy for me, but instead I'm getting this *relentless negativity*.'

'Yeah? Funny, cos the way I heard it, she thinks you've become a tedious groupie with a one-track mind,' Zara said as she handed over the cash for the coffees and they made their way back to the boys.

'No way! Seriously?' Sadie's baby-blue eyes widened in shock. 'I can't *believe* that she would diss me behind my back like that! Talk about two-faced!'

'Yeah, what a nerve. And to think she's meant to be your best friend.'

Sadie, never particularly attuned to irony, nodded enthusiastically. 'You are so right. The main problem with Zara, see, is that she needs a boyfriend. Like, desperately.'

Dear *God*, what she wouldn't give for a decent thunderbolt . . .

Instead, Zara managed to plaster a sickly smile on Fran's face and slammed the tray of drinks down on the table so hard that a wave of coffee splashed upwards on to Rob's T-shirt. He gave a most satisfying yelp. 'Well, it's been loads of fun, guys, but we can't stay here all day chatting. Enjoy your drinks!'

And she grabbed hold of Quinn's arm and hustled him away, leaving the other two staring after them in confusion.

'What was all that about?' Quinn asked. 'And whatever happened to peace, love and my double espresso?'

'I'm sorry. I was hoping it would be a chance for you and Rob to overcome your differences. But Sadie was being really horrible about poor Zara and I just couldn't bear to listen any more . . . Treacherous two-faced cow,' she added bitterly.

'That's what I've always liked about you, Fran: you're so good-hearted. It's sweet of you to stick up for Zara, especially after the way she's picked on you.'

'Yeah, well, I'm sure I deserved it. I can be very irritating at times . . . What do you think of her, anyway?'

Quinn shrugged. 'Zara? She's all right.'

'Just "all right"?'

'Sure, she's fun to hang around with. And she's a good-looking girl, no mistake. But she can be stroppy as hell. You see, I've learned my lesson: I'm beginning to appreciate the appeal of different qualities. *Softer* qualities.'

Zara didn't know what to make of this. Quinn had always been a pro at dazzling girls with his Mr Sensitivity act. But this insistence on being remorseful and self-deprecating was different – and a lot less fun. The longer he kept it up, the more irritated she got, and the harder it became to remember Fran's winsome ways. Which Quinn, apparently, was so keen on. Or was he? Was it just a ruse to get into Ms Roper's big knickers? And if so, should she be relieved that he was the same old scoundrel as before, or royally peeved that a loser like Fran had become the object of his attentions?

It was simpler for Quinn. He hadn't used to be a nice guy and Fran hadn't used to be desirable. Now she was. Fran only went for nice guys. Therefore, as long as Fran was desirable, Quinn would be nice. And he could see his strategy was working. Her odd behaviour this afternoon was surely evidence of her own niceness wavering before the temptations of his . . . Never had the thrill of the chase been quite so unpredictable, or quite so exhilarating . . .

All he needed to do was to keep up the good work. He'd played along with her reconciliation attempt, admired her generosity of spirit as regards the whole Zara thing, and even managed to convey what a caring big brother he was.

Meanwhile, Fran had a faraway look in her eyes. 'Sorry if I seem a little . . . up and down . . . at the moment,' she said. 'I've got a lot on my mind. A lot of things I have to work through . . . about me . . . and Ash . . .'

He knew it! 'I'm sorry to hear that. If there's anything you'd like to talk about, anything I can do to help, just say the word.' Soulful sigh, flirtatious yet reassuring smile. 'But you know what you need right now? Fun. Distraction. Company.'

'Company?'

'Yeah. In fact, I was thinking that you should come round to mine tonight. We could hang out, relax . . . As just good friends, obviously.'

'Obviously,' Zara said demurely. 'A cosy night in with a shoulder to cry on is just what I need right now. And of course, it would be great to get to know your family a little better.'

'Right. I'm, er, sure they'd love to meet you too.'

'Then you've got yourself a date, Mr Adams.'

God, she was good.

But an hour later, Zara's mood was back to its customary black. She'd arrived at the public toilets a couple of streets away from the Unicorn Lounge at twenty past six, the exact time she'd arranged to meet Fran and ten minutes before both transformations were due to wear off. It was the first occasion in her life she'd ever turned up to something on time, and was meant to compensate for some of the afternoon's little misunderstandings. She'd even done quite a good job of taking Fran's body back to its pre-makeover stage; scrubbing away all incriminating traces of scarlet lips or black eyeliner. But her efforts were wasted. Time was nearly up and there was still no sign of the purple-eyed, chestnut-haired super-vamp.

Then at six twenty-seven there came the clippity-clop of high heels as Sabrina rounded the corner at a high-speed totter. Zara nearly choked on her cigarette.

Fran hadn't had the chance to improve on her initial clean-up beside the skip, and so Sabrina was still adorned with globules of meringue and elderly fruit salad. Her dress was half pulled off one shoulder. The purple eyes were wild and staring, and the chestnut mane flying raggedly behind her as she careered down the street.

'No – puff – time to – explain – puff – people after – puff – me –' Fran gasped, Sabrina's bosom heaving like it had never heaved before. Sure enough, a posse of angry-looking blondes was hot on her heels. Christian's fiancée and her friends had come out just as she was limping away from the Unicorn Lounge, and somehow – Fran wasn't quite sure how it had happened – the quarrel had flared up again.

'Back-stabber!' one of them was screeching.

'Gatecrasher!' yelled another.

'You'll pay for wrecking my reception, bitch!' snarled the bride, hitching up her pearly dress so that she could run all the faster.

For once, Zara was lost for words. Fran flung herself through the doorway, grabbing her by the arm and pulling her into a cubicle with only seconds to spare. With trembling hands, she slid the lock behind them just as the vigilante blondes stormed the room and began hammering at the door. The next moment, both of them were overcome with pins and needles all over as a purplish mist descended on their eyes and wrapped itself around their limbs.

'Come on out! We know you're in there!' yelled Christian's fiancée. Somebody else gave the door a kick with the pointed toe of her designer boots.

Fran smoothed her hair, took a deep breath and unlocked the door, the invisible genie treading on her heels.

'Can I help you?' she enquired.

There was a baffled silence. Her former persecutors were all red and shiny in the face, and breathing hard.

'There was a woman,' said one of them belligerently, 'a woman in a black dress with meringue in her hair. You must have seen her – we followed her here.'

'Are you sure?' said Fran as she glanced around the room. It was clear that all the other cubicles were empty, though the bride was still checking behind the doors, presumably on the off-chance that Sabrina had managed to tuck herself behind one of the sanitary bins.

'It's like she's vanished into thin air,' she muttered.

'But we *saw* her go in here,' said one of her henchwoman insistently.

Fran looked at the half-empty champagne bottle under the henchwoman's arm. 'Been to a party?' she asked innocently.

'Yes. So?'

'Oh, nothing . . . I just wondered if maybe all those bubbles have gone to your head . . .'

*

After seeing off Sabrina's lynch mob, both Fran and the genie had laughed hysterically for nearly ten minutes. A lot of it was relief at being back in their own bodies again. 'Phew. It feels good to be me,' Fran said cheerily.

'Same here,' said Zara, admiring her washboard stomach and multiple piercings. 'I'll never take my natural sex appeal for granted again.'

'So how did it go? Any, er, problems?'

'Have a little faith! Like I said, everything was under control. And of course,' Zara added brightly before Fran could follow up with awkward questions, 'the important thing is that *you've* recovered the ring.'

The tale of the charm's recovery took up most of the journey home. Every time Fran paused Zara would jump in with more questions and exclamations of one sort or another. In the normal course of things, this should have made her suspicious, but Fran was still on a celebratory high.

Until, that is, the door to her house was yanked open before she could even put her key in the lock. 'And what have you got to say for yourself?' demanded her mother, grim-faced. 'You have got some serious explaining to do, young lady,' said her father, looming behind.

Zara decided discretion was the better part of valour, and promptly vanished into the ring.

Fran spent the next half-hour shut in the kitchen with her mum and dad while they listed all the different ways and reasons as to why her behaviour that afternoon had been unacceptable. 'The smoking and the drinking were bad enough,' said her mum. 'But to do it while you were supposed to be looking after your little brother and sister – that's what really shocked me.' 'I've just had Mrs Larkin on the phone,' her dad put in, 'telling me that you seemed "erratic and aggressive" and asking if everything was all right at home! What on earth was I supposed to say to that?' 'And then to run off with that Quinn boy when I was trying to talk to you!' her mum exclaimed. 'Is that who you've been with all afternoon?'

'I, um, don't know . . .' mumbled Fran.

'You don't *know*? Well, I'm afraid that's not good enough!'

'I honestly don't know what came over me,' she said helplessly. 'But I'm incredibly sorry. Believe me.'

Mrs Roper put a hand on her arm. 'Look, love,' she said, 'your father and I are very disappointed in your behaviour. But in a way,' her mum continued, 'I'm glad we had that argument. Some of the things you said – about not treating you like a kid, letting you be a normal teenager – well, it made me think. Maybe we have put too much pressure on you to be responsible and sensible at all times. So if your recent, er, performance was an attempt to show us this, perhaps we can all learn something from today.'

Fran looked up at her mum in surprise. 'R-r-really?' she stammered. 'Because whatever happened this afternoon won't happen again. Ever.'

'I'm glad to hear it,' said her dad. 'I don't know what's going on between you and Ash, or you and this Fin or Win or whoever he is, but I want to be able to trust you to do the right thing. Understand?'

'I understand,' said Fran. 'I won't let you down again.' Wearily, she turned to go.

'Oh, and one other thing,' said her mum. 'I found that cat of yours in the street just now. Looks in a right state, but I put him in your bedroom.'

Ash was even more bedraggled than Sabrina. He was walking with a limp, and there was a sickly smell of peaches clinging to his rumpled tufts of fur. A large pink velvet ribbon had been tied around his neck. Its bow was torn and muddied, and stuck up at a lopsided tilt.

'Ash!' cried Fran, sinking to the floor beside him. 'Whatever happened?'

'Tallulah, that's what,' he spat. 'As soon as you left she gave me a bubble bath and this . . . this . . . monstrosity.' He pawed futilely at the ribbon. 'She half-choked and half-drowned me to death! Then, to add insult to injury, she and her little she-demon friends spent most of the afternoon parading me around in a pram. A *pram*! And me, a prince of the royal blood! Never,' he said, every bit of him aquiver with outrage, 'never, in all my years of servitude to the ring, have I been so humiliated.'

'How did you get away?'

'Stuck my claws in her arm.' Ash sniffed. 'You wouldn't believe the fuss – I might as well have chewed her legs off. Her mother was ready to call pest control, but in all the excitement I managed to make my escape . . . Not before I'd taken a small revenge, admittedly.'

'Revenge?'

'I relieved myself on the birthday cake,' he said with dignity. 'Anyhow, I managed to jump into the back of the catering van and then made my way here by bus. Four buses, that is. I got found and thrown out of the first one. Right into the path of the oncoming traffic! It was a miracle I wasn't made into purée of Wonder Cat.'

'Oh, Ash, I'm so sorry.' Fran set to gently removing the ribbon from his neck. 'But your, um, sacrifice was not in vain. Look!' She held up her wrist, from which the curse bracelet and the ring charm dangled. 'Only one to go.'

Of course Ash wanted to hear the whole story, and she got Zara out to help tell it. Fran was pleased to see that the genie actually looked a little sheepish for once. She knew she'd have to have it out with Zara sooner or later, but since her evil twin's exploits had apparently led to some kind of mother-daughter breakthrough, Fran decided the confrontation could wait. For now.

'So, Zara,' she said after she'd related Sabrina's adventures for the second time that evening, 'tell us about your afternoon. If you saw Quinn, I hope that means you were on the track of Daisy and the cat charm.'

'But of course. By the end of our date I had the boy eating out of my hand.' The genie looked slyly at Ash. 'I must say, he seems quite devoted.'

Ash sat bolt upright from where he'd been wolfing down a plate of chicken nuggets.

'In fact,' she continued with relish, 'he says he has his friendship with Fran here to thank for his recent change of character. I believe you've been quite an inspiration to him. Ah, there's nothing like the female touch . . .'

'Get to the point,' Fran said uncomfortably. 'Did you find out anything about the charm or not?'

Zara smiled nastily. 'In a manner of speaking. I've got Daisy's big brother to promise to introduce you – when you go round for a cosy evening at his place tonight.'

'Absolutely not!' said Ash, pacing up and down with his tail lashing, green sparks flashing from his eyes. 'I forbid it!'

Fran stared at him in disbelief. 'Hold on – *you* forbid *me*?'

'It's a question of honour! And propriety!'

'Watch out, Fran,' said Zara, floating up on her side to survey the fun. 'Before you know it, you'll be locked in a basement in a burka.'

'Stay out of this,' Fran snapped, 'you've already meddled enough.' She turned to Ash again. 'I can't believe you don't trust me!'

'*Your* honour, my Purest Lily, my Flame of Righteousness, is beyond reproach. That son of a leprous goatherd is a different matter. Besides –' he muttered something unintelligible. Fran had to lean in to hear him, 'being small, fluffy and feline is bad enough. But sitting on the sidelines unable to defend you is even worse.'

'That's very gallant of you, Ash. But I don't need defending – I can deal with Quinn myself.'

His tail twitched. 'Nonetheless, I don't want you to go. We must find another way to recover the charm.'

'What, and waste all my hard work?' drawled Zara.

Fran ignored her. 'Listen, Ash, this is our best chance. One evening in Quinn's company is nothing – not when we've already faced down Leila and Tallulah and Uncle Stu. Be reasonable.'

There was a long silence.

'Very well, I will let you go. But on one condition.'

'What?' she asked warily.

'That we use one of the wishes as a back-up security measure. To make sure that the camel turd keeps his thoughts pure and his conduct honourable.'

'You want to waste *another* wish? But what if—'

'Please,' said Ash, softly this time. 'Please, Fran. Do it for me. So I won't have to worry.'

He went on to point out that the wish wouldn't be activated as long as Quinn behaved himself. Fran was still feeling uncomfortable on Quinn's behalf – after all, it wasn't exactly his fault if the Zara–Fran hybrid had been sending him come-hither signals all afternoon – but in the end the best she could do was to stipulate that she wouldn't wish for anything involving vats of oil or pits of snakes. And Ash's proposed wording seemed innocuous enough: 'I wish that Quinn would be a perfect gentleman in my company.'

'I know your standards are considerably lower than the rest of civilized society,' Ash informed the genie sternly, 'so you'd better ensure the magic kicks in *before* he requests a naked massage and chocolate body paint.'

*

Quinn was in for another surprise when he found Fran waiting on his doorstep. Instead of the vampy rock chick of the afternoon, this version of Fran was wearing no make-up, had put her hair up in a severe bun and was dressed in a full-length skirt and long-sleeved white blouse buttoned up to the neck. Before he could even open his mouth, she held up a hand and started to speak.

'I wasn't myself this afternoon. You should therefore ignore anything I did or said which struck you as out of character. For this I apologize. Furthermore, you have previously given me to understand that all you want from me is friendship, so if I gave you the impression that this evening would be some kind of romantic date, I will make it clear to you now that that impression was wrong. Do we understand one another?'

'Absolutely,' said Quinn, with a lingering smile. Fran's clipped tones didn't put him off; in fact he thought her innocent convent-girl get-up was rather sexy. Especially after he'd glimpsed the feisty rebel inside, just waiting to be unleashed. He imagined releasing her silky hair from its pins, unfastening those little pearly buttons one by one . . .

He led Fran into the house. Careful not to look as if he'd made any sort of effort, he was wearing a heather-coloured T-shirt and battered jeans. Battered designer jeans, that is, and T-shirt that clung snugly to his tall frame. 'You want a drink?'

'No thanks. Is your sister around?'

Jeez, what was this obsession with Daisy? 'Not

for much longer. She and Magda are going to the cinema.'

The next moment, Daisy herself came down the stairs, her mournful-looking au pair trailing behind her.

Even at the age of ten, Daisy Adams was already well on her way to following in her brother's foot-steps as a professional heartbreaker. She had the same chocolate-brown eyes and delectable cheek-bones and, what's more, the same expression of martyrdom that Quinn was presently cultivating.

When she caught sight of her brother, her tragic expression intensified. 'I'm still not talking to you!' she said. '*You're* the stupid reason stupid Tallulah wouldn't let me come to her stupid party! There were going to be gift bags from Selfridges and *everything*!'

Quinn had forgotten Daisy was in a mood with him because he wouldn't go to some kiddie party of a mate of hers. The little brat better not show him up. 'I'm sorry, Day. I'll make it up to you.' He hoped Daisy would see past his tender brotherly smile to the threat behind it. 'This is Fran, by the way. She's a – a friend from school.'

'Hello,' Daisy said without any enthusiasm.

'Hi,' said Fran distractedly, straining for signs of an ancient Arabian artefact. Some kind of animal, probably, but not necessarily a cat . . . Would Daisy wear it as a pendant, or on a bracelet? She had a rope of multicoloured beads around her neck and was wearing a watch but no bracelet. Maybe she'd put the charm in her jewellery box. Or lost it. Or passed it on to somebody else. Or thrown it away. She could ask to go and see the kid's bedroom, but that would come across as a bit creepy, wouldn't it?

'Fran's got a brother only a bit younger than you,' Quinn told his sister. 'He's been in all sorts of TV adverts and stuff. Isn't that right, Fran? Er – Fran?'

But Fran's eyes were fixed on Daisy's denim bag. The strap was adorned by one of those bag charms that were all over the shops right now, and there, among the glass beads and the feather and the mini teddy bear, was a tiny metal animal. From where she was standing, it could be any four-legged creature, but it was unmistakably part of the curse bracelet. Yesss! She gave a small whoop.

Daisy stared. 'The film starts at six thirty, so we have to go – unless you've got any more *friends* you'd like me to meet,' she said to her brother pointedly.

Fran saw her chance to get the charm slipping away. 'Wait!' she exclaimed. 'We'll come too. In fact, we can take you instead of, er, Magda. That would be all right with you, wouldn't it, Magda?'

The au pair's long-suffering expression brightened considerably. Quinn, however, looked confused. 'I thought you wanted a quiet night in.'

'Yeah, but I haven't been to the cinema in ages! What are you going to see, Daisy?'

'*Dance of the Penguins*. It's this really sweet drama-doc about—'

'I know! A poor little penguin looking for his mum! Perfect – heart-warming *and* educational! Please, Quinn, can we go?'

'Uh . . . OK. I guess. If that's what you really want.'

In the normal course of things, there was no way Quinn Adams would waste his time and cash on some lame animal flick, even if it was to please a girl. And his fail-safe seduction scheme was already set up: the slouchy sofa barely big enough for two, dimmed lights, soft music, the key to his parents' drinks cabinet . . . But then again, the back row of a darkened cinema was not without its opportunities. Clearly, Fran was still struggling to suppress her powerful feelings for him. Poor girl, he thought indulgently, she'd feel so much better once she gave up and gave in.

Fran's hopes of making progress with the charm en route to the cinema were thwarted by Daisy taking the last seat on the bus, while she and Quinn had to stand a little way down in the aisle. Still, she wasn't too disheartened. After her experiences with Tallulah and Lily, Fran had decided against the straightforward request strategy. Theft seemed to be the simplest option. And since the charm was only attached to Daisy's bag by a bit of pink ribbon, Fran was fairly confident she could 'liberate' it under cover of darkness during the film, or perhaps distract her target in the popcorn queue.

In the meantime, however, there was Quinn to take care of. 'So,' she tried, over the rumbling of the bus, 'how's it going?'

'Not too bad, thanks to you. You're a very good influence.'

'I find that hard to believe.' Not for the first time,

Fran wished she knew exactly what Zara had got up to that afternoon.

'Seriously – all that stuff you said about peace and reconciliation and letting bygones be bygones made a big impression on me. So after you left I went back to find Rob and had things out with him. Man to man, y'know? I think we both feel a lot better for it.'

Zara, an ambassador for peace? Fran could hardly believe her ears. 'That's great news. It must have been hard for you, being cut off from your friends like that,' she said wistfully.

Quinn was encouraged by her despondent expression. After they got off the bus and joined the queue for the cinema, he took the plunge. 'How's Ash, by the way? You mentioned you were having . . . problems.'

'He's fine, thanks. We're both fine. Everything's fine. Absolutely one hundred per cent fine, in fact.'

'That's cool.' Fran had sounded delightfully unconvincing. 'He seems like a nice bloke. Though I can't help thinking that there's more to him than meets the eye.'

'Ash was just brought up differently to most people around here, that's all.'

'Ah yes,' said Quinn, nodding wisely, 'love across the divide.'

'What do you mean by that?'

'Not a divide,' he amended. 'More like . . . an information gap. Like I said, he's a good guy. Probably. It's just he's just a bit of mystery – I'm sure you've heard the rumours.'

'No,' said Fran through gritted teeth.

'Oh. Well, I don't want to upset you, and you know what school gossip is like . . .'

'Get to the point.'

Quinn made a show of great reluctance. 'OK . . . here goes . . . the thing is, Fran, I heard a rumour that he already has a girlfriend. Well, wife. *Wives*, that is. Back in Baghdad.'

Fran gave a snort of laughter. But then she realized that Quinn had turned to the woman behind him. '. . . I'm sure it's just bitchy gossip,' he was saying earnestly, 'but I thought you should know. Just in case you really were running around with a married man.'

The woman turned pale. '*Neil?*' she gasped, turning to the older man waiting next to her. 'Is this true?'

Neil shot a murderous look in Quinn's direction. 'Outrageous! I've never seen this kid before in my life,' he blustered. 'I'll have you know,' he said, jabbing a finger at him, 'there's laws against slander like that. Me and Denise have never actually—'

'*Denise?* Who the hell is Denise?' demanded his companion. Neil opened and shut his mouth, but all that came out was an inarticulate croaking sound. 'No – on second thoughts, I don't want to know,' she snapped. 'I've already heard enough.'

She flounced out of the cinema lobby, Neil stumbling behind and begging her to wait. Quinn stared after them in disbelief.

'What was all that about? I don't understand . . . why did that woman think I was talking about her? And how come I—'

'God knows,' said Fran. 'They must have overheard our conversation and got the wrong end of the stick.'

So Ash's wish wasn't quite as innocuous as it had appeared: it seemed that Quinn's less 'gentlemanly' remarks were rebounding off her and on to their neighbours. Still, there wasn't much she could do about it, except for making extra sure she nipped any flirtation in the bud. And, of course, the sooner she got the charm the sooner it would all be over.

Speaking of which . . . While Quinn went to the snack counter, Fran headed to where Daisy was waiting. She smiled ingratiatingly. 'Hey, Daisy, how about some popcorn? Or an ice cream? Ooh, I know – pick 'n' mix! Mm! How about I hold your bag while you get what you want?'

Daisy gave her an odd look and backed away. She was used to being sucked up to by girls who wanted to get in with her brother, but this Fran person was even more desperate than most. Plus, she was dressed like a particularly uncool school teacher. Her big brother was definitely letting his standards slip.

'The film's about to start,' she said shortly. 'I'm going to get a seat.'

'Yeah! Great! Good idea,' said Fran, hastening after her.

Quinn brought up the rear, shooting a disgusted look at the *Dance of the Penguins* poster they passed on the way. 'Your heart will melt quicker than the polar ice caps!' the strapline promised. Just to rub it in, next to it was an advert for *Mutant Death Fiends III*. Now, *that* was more like it: faced with widescreen

Death Fiends, a softy like Fran would be trembling in his manly arms within the first three minutes.

But in the event, his manly arms didn't even manage to steer Fran into the back row. She also resisted Quinn's proposal that they should sit a few seats away from his sister. 'We can't leave her on her own, Quinn! It would be really irresponsible.'

Her flushed face and flustered demeanour, however, revealed just how irresponsible she longed to be. Quinn decided to crank up the temptation.

'Here,' he said, as the trailers began, 'sweets for the sweet.' He smiled flirtatiously as he reached to feed Fran a treat from his pick 'n' mix –

– and found himself cramming a wad of marshmallow against the mouth of the middle-aged man to his left. It was difficult to tell which of the two of them was more shocked.

'Er, I'm r-really s-sorry,' stammered Quinn, hand frozen about a centimetre from the stranger's mouth. He couldn't think how it, or he, had got there. 'I, uh, thought you were someone else.'

The man stared at him incredulously, then got up and moved to another row.

Now it was Quinn's turn to be flustered. 'God, I don't know what happened there,' he muttered to Fran. 'Something really weird is going on.'

Fran shrugged nervously. Her misgivings increased yet further when the newly vacant seat to Quinn's left was taken by a young woman with green dreadlocks. Her tie-dyed T-shirt read 'Eco-Warriors Do It Better' and she had a Zara-style spike through her nose.

'Never mind. Let's just sit back and enjoy the film, OK?'

The trailers had ended at last, and the cinema audience let out a collective 'awwww' as a crowd of fluffy baby penguins waddled into view. A famous Hollywood heart-throb was doing the voice-over. 'Join me,' he said earnestly, 'for an epic story of survival, as Pickles the Penguin takes his first steps into a cold, cold world . . .'

Meanwhile, Fran was trying – via surreptitious prodding with her feet – to find out where Daisy had stashed her bag. She leaned towards the floor on the pretext of looking in her own bag, and felt around under the seats. In the process, she brushed against Quinn's ankle.

'Seems like you just can't keep your hands off me,' he said teasingly.

His eco-warrior neighbour gave him a look that could have taken out a whole army of Mutant Death Fiends.

'I'll thank you to keep your pervy comments to yourself.'

'Hey, I *never*—'

'Shhhh!' went their entire row.

After a brief – and on Quinn's part, baffled – pause, Fran decided it was time to make an intervention. 'Listen,' she whispered to him urgently, 'you said you only want to be friends. That means no compliments and no cheesy comments. Please. It's for your own good, believe me.'

Quinn barely heard her. He was too preoccupied with trying to work out exactly what was going on. After a while he looked up to see Fran staring at him anxiously, and oblivious to the piece of toffee popcorn stuck to an errant strand of her hair. Her long, silky hair. Hair that would feel deliciously soft wrapped around his finger . . .

'Here, let me.' He went to brush the popcorn off. And found he was running his hands through his neighbour's dreadlocks.

'URGH!' they both yelped.

'Shhhhhh!' went the entire cinema.

'You'd better tell your boyfriend to quit molesting me,' the eco-warrior said to Fran in a vicious undertone. 'Else I'm calling security.'

'He's not my boyfriend—'

'I am not molesting—'

'Will you shut *up*!' hissed Daisy, reaching over to thump Quinn with her bag.

At which point – like magic, like fate, like the best of all possible luck – the charm slid off its flimsy pink ribbon and into Fran's lap.

But now was not the time for celebrations. The last thing Quinn was capable of right now was sitting in silence. The more he thought about recent developments, the more freaked out he started to feel. The world had gone mad. Or he had. He was probably suffering from mental blackouts – as he kept on trying to explain to Fran.

'Forget about it,' she said.

'I can't,' Quinn whispered back.

'You have to. Focus on the penguins.'

'Sod the penguins!'

He'd voiced his frustration louder than he'd realized. Much louder. In fact, his ungentlemanly expletive was still echoing around the auditorium. Goaded past all endurance, the eco-warrior dumped her tub of cheesy nachos all over his head.

Nor was that the last excitement of the evening. After they had fled the cinema, Daisy – in hysterics – had phoned home, demanding to be picked up. Ten minutes later, Magda came to the rescue in a taxi, but Daisy was adamant Quinn wasn't getting into it. She was never speaking to him again. She'd never be able to see a penguin without feeling sick. He was the worst brother in the world and it would serve him right if he ended up going out with a girl like *her*.

At this, she had shot Fran a look of loathing, which Fran returned with a cheery grin. She was feeling genuinely upbeat. After all, she had the charm.

But fate had another surprise in store. While Fran waited for Quinn to clean himself up in the toilets of a burger bar, her eye glanced over a discarded newspaper.

Was that *Leila*?

Fran snatched it up for a closer look. The tabloid was open on the showbiz gossip section and, incredibly, a blurry photo of the Queen of Darkness getting out of a cab. Next to it was a still of Posy Parkin and Zed Boulder in action on *Hype!*. 'POSY IN MELTDOWN!' gasped the headline.

The entertainment world is reeling after the shock departure of Posy Parkin from hit weekend show

Hype!. *A spokesman for the show confirmed that Ms Parker is suffering from 'celebrity exhaustion'. As yet, no date has been set for her return. In the meantime, unknown starlet Leila Arrabiata will be taking her place alongside co-host Zed Boulder. Last night, Ms Parkin was unavailable for comment but—*

'What are you reading?' Quinn had finally appeared from the toilets. He'd shoved his head and shoulders under a tap and was now dripping dolefully. 'Oh, that thing with Posy Parkin. It was on the radio this morning.'

Fran was remembering Leila watching the TV on Friday. Her own flip words echoed in her head: a *goddess, according to some people* . . . 'I can't believe it,' she whispered. 'It's my fault.'

'What's your fault? Are you feeling OK? You've gone white.'

Somehow she managed to pull herself together. Whatever was going on with Posy and Leila would just have to wait. She stuffed the newspaper page into her pocket and managed a weak smile. 'I'm fine – how about you?'

'Nacho-free. My hair still whiffs of cheese though.'

Fran grimaced, remembering Sabrina and the food fight. She'd got off lightly: smelling of fruit salad was way better than processed cheddar.

'I just don't understand what the hell is going on,' Quinn said for the fiftieth time that evening. 'I keep losing control of myself and it's freaking me out. Like I've been *possessed*.'

'It could be that you're just a bit, um, stressed,'

Fran suggested as they began to head back to Milson Road. 'People do odd things when they're nervous.'

He looked at her in surprise. 'But I never get nervous!' Then he paused. 'Though when it comes to you, maybe I should.'

Fran laughed uneasily.

'I don't mean anything bad by it. Just . . . well, when I'm with you, strange things keep happening.'

Quinn stopped and turned to look at her, a serious expression in his dark eyes. His ragged blond hair had darkened with the water, and the droplets were gleaming in the street light. Fran had a sudden, piercingly vivid image of Ash in the rain, on an evening very like this one.

Then he reached out and lightly stroked the skin on her arm. 'And strangest of all, I don't really mind. There's something special about you, you see, something . . . magical.'

Fran blushed. By rights, his stroking of her arm, and the cheesy compliment, should have rebounded on to one of the other passers-by. Did that mean that, for once, Quinn was being sincere?

'Look, Quinn,' she said gently, 'maybe some things just aren't meant to be. Though I'm sorry if tonight was . . . difficult for you.'

'That's OK. It's probably good for me to make an idiot of myself once in a while. Stop me getting too cocky, y'know?' He smiled wryly.

'Hey, it wasn't all bad. At least I got some toffee popcorn out of it.'

'I suppose the evening hasn't been a total disaster then,' he said, smiling at her. They were outside her door.

* * * * * ✦ 125 ★ * * * * *

'Not at all,' said Fran, smiling back.

'I just hope that crazy boyfriend of yours knows how lucky he is,' said Quinn as he leaned in for a farewell kiss . . .

For a long time afterwards, Mr Roper never missed an opportunity to tell the story of the night when he'd opened the front door, only to be greeted with a smack on the lips from one of Fran's boyfriends. Fran didn't ever come up with a satisfactory explanation, though at the time she had flashed her dad a feeble smile and muttered something about 'Italian ancestry – he's always very demonstrative', before hurrying up to her bedroom, where Ash was impatiently pacing the floor.

'Don't start,' she warned him as soon as she closed the door. 'Yes, I got the charm and, yes, my "honour" is intact.'

'Hah! Then I take it the wish came in useful after all.' Ash inclined his head towards the window. 'That *was* Quinn I saw just now, bolting off down the street as if the Hounds of Hades were after him?'

'Never you mind,' Fran replied. Ash's smug tone annoyed her. 'We've got bigger issues to deal with – it seems your ex has kept some tricks up her sleeve.'

She fetched Zara from out of the ring and presented the newspaper to them both.

'No doubt about it, the girl's got style,' the genie said with an admiring shake of her head. 'From flying rugs to red carpets in one easy step.'

Ash flicked his tail impatiently. 'Style's got nothing to do with it. I assume Leila is responsible for Ms Parkin's downfall?'

'A dead cert, I reckon,' said Fran. 'But what I'm worried about is how that downfall was achieved.'

'Oh, that's easy,' said Zara, with an airy wave of her hand. 'Blackmail. All you'd have to do is plant drugs in her dressing room, or find a D-list celeb willing to spill the beans about three-in-a-bed romps and rubber fetishes.'

'Or you could keep things simple and try a nice quick curse.'

'What d'you mean?'

Fran went to fetch Leila's bracelet from its hiding place and laid it out on her bed. Axe, pimply hand, demonic face, poison bottle, the ring and the beast . . . She hadn't liked to examine them too closely before, unsettled by their strange blend of the alluring and the sinister. Although Daisy's charm was barely two centimetres long, the detailing of the metal was so intricate you could see that the animal's teeth were bared and its fur standing on end.

Now it was time for a stocktake. After she attached the new charm to a link by its little hook, she held the bracelet up to the light, examining it bit by bit. Just as she'd feared, there was a tiny loop of wire sticking out from one of the links near the clasp. A missing hook for a missing charm.

'See?' She showed the others. 'There should be seven. The magic number. And though I don't know what the seventh curse does, I bet you anything Posy's been the recipient.'

'Fact is,' said Zara bitterly, 'that two-faced cheating snake never meant for us to break the spells.'

For a while everyone was too depressed to speak.

Leila had told Fran that the bracelet needed to be complete to reverse the curses, all the while keeping one of the charms back. She'd sent them off on a fool's errand.

'Well,' said Ash at last, slowly and wearily, 'it's not a total disaster. As long as she's still here, we've got a chance of getting the seventh charm. And we know exactly where she'll be tomorrow: hosting *Hype!* from two until four. We'll just have to use one of our wishes to get to her.'

'The sooner the better.' Fran reached for her mobile. 'I guess I'd better give Amira a call to thank her for covering for me this afternoon. Looks like we might need her to do the same tomorrow.'

Zara cleared her throat. 'Erm, about you and Amira. There's just one small problem . . .'

Zara wasn't best known for her persuasive skills, preferring to rely on coercion and threats of violence, but the following explanation was a masterclass in the art of spin. According to the genie, Amira had taken one look at her and Quinn and jumped to a number of insulting conclusions. Zara, naturally, had done her best to act in an appropriately Fran-like manner, spreading sweetness and light all around. 'All I said was that it was time her feud with Quinn was brought to an amicable conclusion,' she said virtuously. 'Just like I tried to get Quinn and Rob to do the whole kiss 'n' make-up thing. But that girl was determined to see things in the worst possible light. Talk about overreaction! She's got a vicious temper on her, you know.' And then she had shaken her head in a sorrowful manner. 'Somebody needed to take a stand.'

Fran wasn't fooled. It was true Amira had a short temper, and she knew that the sight of Fran apparently enjoying a love-in with her ex – when she was supposed to be in the midst of a personal trauma – would have been like a red rag to a bull. But she was in no doubt that Zara had made the worst of a bad situation.

'Guess I'd better start grovelling,' she said, tight-lipped, as she picked up the phone. She wasn't entirely surprised to find Amira wasn't answering. Neither was Zoë, nor Parminder. With growing trepidation, she tried Naz.

On the fifth ring, she got an answer of sorts. There was a mumbling from the other end, a crackle of static, and the sound of footsteps.

'Hello?'

'Fran,' came a whisper down the other end of the phone. 'We're not supposed to be talking to you.'

'Please, Naz, whatever Amira thinks happened this afternoon, I can explain. There's absolutely *nothing* going on with me and Quinn.'

'Yeah? So what about tonight?'

'Tonight?'

'Zoë's brother went past the cinema. Said he saw you and Quinn going in together.'

'That's only because Quinn is . . . helping me. Helping me get something.'

'Like what?'

'Er . . . it's a secret.'

'Riiiight. A secret that involves going behind Ash's back with your best friend's slimy ex.'

'No! That's not it at all! Honestly, Naz, I'd love to tell you what's going on, it's just that . . . I can't. Not right now. But if I could just talk to Amira, maybe come round and—'

'Look, Fran, I'm sorry, but I think it's better if you stay away for a while. Give her some time to cool down.' Naz sighed. 'I just hope this big secret of yours is worth it.' And she put the phone down.

Fran stared at the screen in a daze of shock.

'I take it you just lost your alibi,' drawled the genie.

It was the final straw. Fran rounded on her furiously. 'You!' she exploded. 'You! This is all *your* fault! *Everything* is your fault!' Zara bobbed a metre up into the air in alarm and found she was backed, still floating, into a corner. 'If you hadn't barged into that shop yesterday with your stupid comments we wouldn't even be in this mess in the first place! You don't *deserve* to be let out of that ring. In fact, next time I see Leila I'm going to ask her to put an extra seven curses on you to make sure you *never* get out of it. Ever.'

All the nasty comments, the sniping and under-mining and goading . . . Every time, no matter how much she longed to retaliate, Fran had held herself back. She had kept telling herself she needed to save her energies for more important things. It was up to her to keep the peace, to act for the greater good, blah blah blah. And now she'd had enough. No more Ms Nice Girl. 'All you've done since we got into this mess is to make everything worse!' she hissed.

Zara pushed herself off the wall, shooting her

body up and along the ceiling, then down again so that she was standing behind Fran's back. Fran whipped round to find the genie glaring, just in front of her nose.

'So the worm's finally turning, is she?' Zara sneered. 'Good. It's about time you stopped trying to act like we're in some cosy little kiddie show where all we need to do is work together and overcome our differences before the slushy group hug at the end. I don't like you. You don't like me. Pretending anything else is a load of hypocritical crud.'

'Honourable and Impassioned Ladies—' began Ash.

'Stay out of this, Cat Boy,' the genie spat. 'This is between me and Roper.'

Fran could agree with this, at least. 'I wasn't asking for a group hug,' she retorted, 'just grudging cooperation. Instead, it's like you're out to sabotage my *entire life*.'

'Sabotage, huh? Let's not forget: *you're* the one who wasted a wish for totally selfish ends just to make your own life easier. You think it was a breeze, walking around in your lumpy carcass for the afternoon? You reckon *you* could successfully impersonate *me* at a moment's notice?'

'That's not the point—'

'Of course it is! In case you hadn't noticed, we're about as opposite as two people could be. Even so, I tried. I really did. OK, so I didn't do things one hundred per cent your way, but the way I see it, I ended up doing everyone a favour. Your parents *do* treat you like you're fifteen going on fifty. That crazy Amira chick *does* need to stop banging on about her persecution complex. I even got Quinn and Rob to get over their stupid feuding. And to top it all, I set things up so you could get your hands on the cat charm. Think about it, Roper. Maybe a little gratitude is in order.'

They stood centimetres apart, breathing hard. Fran was still seething but on some level, Zara's words had hit home. She forced herself to calm down, draw back and speak with a semblance of control.

'All right then. So where do you suggest we go from here?'

'I suggest you grant me a wish, as previously agreed –'

'*What?* No frigging *way*—'

'– and I use it to ensure you get to the *Hype!* recording.'

There had to be a catch. 'You're spending your wish on getting me a ticket? I don't understand.'

'In all the excitement, I guess you've forgotten Mr and Mrs Moron are off to *Hype!* this weekend. I propose using a wish to ensure you take Sadie's place – killing two birds with one thunderbolt, you might say.'

Fran looked at her narrowly. 'How does getting hold of Sadie's ticket fit into your private wish-making agenda?'

Zara smiled evilly. 'Oh, I can think of several entertaining possibilities.'

'It's not about *entertainment*. Remember: once those last two wishes are gone, you'll be stuck in that ring until it finds a new owner. On the plus side, you won't ever see me again, but I don't reckon you'll enjoy being bossed around by some stranger either.'

'We all know what the risks are – and that didn't stop you and Ali Baba throwing away wishes right, left and centre.' Zara screwed up her face in disgust. 'Admit it: you both wasted them for selfish reasons, but now I'm claiming my share – in a way that will work to everyone's advantage – you come all high and mighty on me. Talk about double standards!'

But Fran did not want to talk about double standards. She'd had enough of the whole conversation. Instead, she sent the genie packing with an angry twist of the ring.

'Can you believe her nerve?' she exploded to Ash, as soon as they were alone. 'As if I'd waste a wish on her pathetic schemes after she spent the whole afternoon screwing me over!'

'Actually, I think she has a point,' he said from the corner where he'd been grooming his fur for the duration of the argument. 'We'll need to spend a wish to get close to Leila, so if Zara's wish will accomplish this I don't see any harm in keeping to your original bargain. After all, we'll still have a wish left as back-up. I appreciate you're hacked off about her meddling, but really Fran, what did you expect? Asking Zara to take your place among your friends and family! Let's face it, it wasn't exactly your smartest move.'

Fran stared at him in disbelief. She'd taken his support for granted. 'Yeah, well, we'd have *two* wishes for back-up if you hadn't come over all self-righteous and vengeful with poor Quinn.'

'*Poor* Quinn, is it? That wish would never have

been activated if he'd behaved in a gentlemanly fashion.'

'Oh for God's sake! It's not like he tried to abduct me for his harem or exchange me for a camel or whatever you and your mates used to get up to in the Good Old Days.'

'Trust a woman to dredge up grievances of several hundred years ago!'

'At times like this, I can see why Leila's got such a downer on you!'

'Maybe the two of you should set up house together then. Then you can bitch and moan to your heart's content—'

'You know what, maybe we should. Go on, scram! Scat, cat!' She yanked open the door to shoo him out.

'Fran! That poor animal! He looks scared witless!' Her mum was at the top of the stairs, come to see what all the noise was about. 'For goodness sake, what on earth are you shouting about? And really, do you *have* to have your stereo on so loud so late in the evening? You've woken Beth up with all your racket!'

'The cat was making a nuisance of itself,' Fran growled. Ash hissed in reply, then stalked off downstairs, nose in the air.

'I see. Well, hopefully Ash will be back soon and will be able to look after his pet for himself.'

This was exactly the last thing Fran wanted to hear. She blinked and found her eyes filling with tears – of frustration and loneliness and sheer exhaustion. Before she knew it, she'd let out a sob.

'There, there love,' her mum said comfortingly,

pulling her into a hug. 'It's been quite a day, hasn't it? But it's over now and, you know, the old cliché is always true – things *do* look better in the morning.'

'It's not over yet,' Fran mumbled into her shoulder. She sniffed. 'I'm just so tired of trying to hold everything together . . . And me and Ash . . .'

Her mum drew back to look at her. 'If he's hurt you in any way,' she said sternly, 'any way at all—'

'No! No. I know you and Dad don't really like Ash—'

'Now, Fran, that's not true—'

'Yes it is! You think he's cocky and flashy and frivolous! With dodgy shirts and an even dodgier past! But there's so much more to him than that and I really, really, *really* want him back. I want things back to how they used to be.' Fran was crying in earnest now. And she let her mum lead her over to her bed, and undress her as if she was a little girl, as if she was Beth, and tuck her up and bring her hot chocolate and tell her not to worry, because everything was going to be all right.

The following morning Fran called a conference with Zara and Ash in the garden shed. Her mum had been right, she did feel better after a night's sleep; but there was no doubt the atmosphere in the shed was slightly strained. Zara was no more or less unpleasant than usual, but Fran, who didn't share the genie's natural-born relish for slanging matches, was still feeling shaken up by their confrontation. As for Ash, they both carried on as if last night's row had never happened, but things definitely weren't right between them.

Normally after one of their arguments, Fran would reach for Ash's hand, or he'd sling an arm round her shoulder or give her one of his secret looks from under his lashes . . . Exchanging flirtatious looks with a cat, however, was a step too far. *Way* too far. Up till now, Fran hadn't appreciated how much of their relationship – any relationship, in fact – was conducted through body language. It might be more mature to sort out a problem by talking it through in a civilized fashion, but Fran and Ash had always preferred the short cut to making up: a big snog.

Fran thought back to Ash's parting shot about setting up house with his ex. It was ridiculous, as well as insulting, to suggest she had anything in common with Leila, but what if they weren't able to sort out this mess? Would it leave her as bitter and twisted as the princess? The way things were going, she might well be fated to turn into a crazy, lonely old lady who spent her time talking to cats . . .

'I hope you've taken the time to consider my proposal,' said Zara, cutting in on these dismal thoughts. 'Though of course, you being such a fine upstanding citizen and everything, I'm sure you'll do the right thing and honour your side of the deal.'

'I don't need lectures on citizenship from the likes of you, thank you very much,' Fran retorted. 'And before I agree to anything, I want to know exactly what this wish will involve, and how Sadie fits into—'

She was interrupted by the ringing of her mobile. She didn't recognize the number and was about to switch it off, when Zara leaned over to inspect the screen. 'Talk of the she-devil . . . That's Sadie's number, you know. Why ever would she want to call you?'

Fran was equally nonplussed and, despite herself, curious. 'Hello?' she said dubiously.

'Franny!' squealed the voice down the other end. 'Are you surprised to get a call from me?'

'Er, yes, actually.'

'Well, I feel we totally bonded yesterday. Like I finally got to know the *real* you. And you know what? You're not nearly so much of a loser as I thought you were! Isn't that fab?'

Fran didn't know exactly what had gone on between Sadie and her evil twin, but if Sadie was impressed by the encounter she knew it was unlikely to have been anything good. 'Yes, fabulous. Look, Sadie, I'm kind of in the middle of something here so—'

Sadie prattled on as if she hadn't spoken. 'You know me and Robbie have got tickets to the recording of *Hype!* this afternoon, right?'

Fran held up a hand to shush Ash and Zara, who were both demanding to know what was going on. 'Yeah, someone had mentioned it. Lucky you.'

'Lucky? It's the most awesome thing *ever*! Robbie's sister's boyfriend got them for us. He works on the show. You see, Robbie's not only majorly hot, he's also really well connected. And talented. And totally into me . . . Anyway, my olds are away this weekend, and I was thinking you should come over to help me get ready for the big event. Girlie bonding and all that. You can even help me paint my nails.' Sadie paused to let the magnificence of this offer sink in.

'Sounds fun,' said Fran eventually.

'I know! So, I'll see you in half an hour, OK? Sixty-four Elm Avenue.'

'Er—'

'It's gonna be *great*!'

And Sadie rang off.

'What was all that about?' Ash asked.

'I'm not sure. For some reason, Sadie wants me on cheerleading duty – psyching her up for her big TV debut this afternoon. Apparently if I'm really lucky, I get to help choose her nail polish.'

Zara gave a disgusted snort. 'Favour indeed. Amazing what my few hours as the new, improved Fran has done for your street cred – I *told* you you should be grateful . . . Still, at least the timing's good.'

'Good for what?'

'Duh. If you're already at Sadie's on suck-up service, you'll be in prime position for making my wish.'

Fran groaned and put her head in her hands.

Sadie was still in her nightie when Fran arrived, but, true to form, her make-up was intact and her hair blow-dried to gleaming blonde perfection. She opened the door wearing a skimpy satin slip printed all over with hearts, and fluffy pink teddy-bear slippers.

'Franny!' she squeaked adorably, pulling her into

a vanilla-perfume-scented hug. 'I'm so excited you could make it! We're going to have the best girl-time *ever*.'

Fran eyed her warily. Even in the heady days of the Francesca-Sadie-Zara triumvirate, her own presence had only ever been barely tolerated. Still, she wasn't feeling grateful to the genie for her new-found popularity– especially as experience told her that the cutsier Sadie appeared, the more dangerous her agenda. The teddy-bear slippers were probably a bad sign.

'Hi, Sadie. Hope you don't mind, but I've brought my cat along. I'm trying to work the Paris Hilton look – pets as accessories.'

'Oh. You know, Fran, I gotta say, carrying your pet in a handbag is an itsy bit D-list these days. I'm not sure Paris even has that tiny Chewbacca thing any more.'

'Chihuahua.'

'Whatever.' Sadie was examining Fran with a winsome expression. 'Still, I have to approve of the initiative. I can see you're trying. And at the end of the day, that's what counts.'

'Sorry, but what am I trying exactly?'

'To break into the fringes of cool, of course! And I want you to know I am one hundred per cent behind you! Go, girlfriend!' Sadie went to high-five her with an enthusiastic whoop.

Fran fumbled the high five, but decided to take it as an invitation to come in. She was still feeling unsure of why exactly she'd been invited over, but she might as well make the most of it. Perhaps she wouldn't have to use a wish after all – hers *or* Zara's.

There was a chance Sadie would have the ticket lying around somewhere and Fran could just, well, steal it. Or she could slip something into Sadie's drink – nothing *really* bad, a laxative maybe – that would mean she'd be too ill to go. Then if she did a good enough sucking-up job beforehand, Sadie might even give her the ticket of her own free will . . . Anything could happen.

They started off in the kitchen, where Sadie fixed them up with mugs of hot chocolate and a plate of low-calorie snack bars – 'I'm lucky with my metabolism, but I know you must be watching your weight' – before ushering her upstairs to her bedroom. This was pretty much as Fran had expected: a shrine to all things girlish, fuzzy-edged and pink, lit by ropes of fairy lights, and smelling of vanilla body spray. There was even a shelf of immaculately attired Barbie dolls that looked as if they had never been played with, and were a million miles away from the cripples with shorn hair and graffitied faces that Beth had inherited from Fran. The only sign, in fact, that this was the room of a teenager was the wall dedicated to photographs of Rob Crawford in action with the Morons. From the other three walls, a gallery of famous blondes simpered from poster frames: Marilyn Monroe, Reese Witherspoon, Princess Di, Sandy from *Grease* . . .

Fran sat down on a beanbag resembling a giant marshmallow, sinking so deep into its folds that she found herself surveying the scene from an uncomfortable sprawl. She took a sip of the hot chocolate. It was teeth-flinchingly sweet. For a moment, a fleeting vision of Zara's natural habitat swum before her eyes. Probably some black-draped dungeon, the Barbies and teddy bears replaced with voodoo dolls and thumbscrews.

Meanwhile, Sadie pranced over to the big white-painted wardrobe and began flinging armfuls of clothes on to the bed. 'So,' she prattled, 'I want to look extra foxy for Robbie of course, but I need something that will show up well on screen – make me stand out from the crowd, you know? Then they say the camera adds ten pounds, so it's also got to be super-slimming. I was thinking my skinny jeans and one of these.'

She held up a selection of tops. All of them were variants on skimpy, sparkly and pastel-coloured.

OK, so this was easy. 'I'd go for the pink one. I think it's your colour.'

'Yeah, but is it the *right* pink? That's the issue. People don't realize that pink is actually a very tricky colour to wear. It's got these, like, hidden depths.' Sadie began wriggling into the jeans, carelessly flinging off her nightie to reveal a wisp of chiffon bra. It was at this point that Fran noticed Ash was looking a bit *too* comfortably ensconced on the rug beside her.

'Just a minute,' she said, scooping up the cat and dumping him – hissing indignantly – outside the door. 'I could feel my allergy coming on,' she said in explanation as she retuned to the beanbag. 'Sorry about that. You were saying something about the philosophy of pink . . .'

'Actually, I'm not sure pink is, like, appropriate for *Hype!*. A lot of the guests there look kinda, you know, *edgy* . . . So maybe I need a different approach. Break the mould, push the boundaries a bit?'

'Um, powder blue's always nice.'

'Just what I was thinking! We are *totally* soul-mates!' Sadie began to exchange her floaty pink number for something identical in blue. 'The thing is though,' she continued, voice muffled by the material she was pulling over her head, 'I didn't really get you here to talk about clothes.'

'You didn't?'

'No. You see, Fran, hon,' Sadie said, sitting back down on her satin counterpane and fixing her with dewy eyes, 'I've been thinking about you a *lot*, recently. Considering who you are, where you're going . . . And then after our little chat yesterday, everything sorta fell into place.'

Fran made what she hoped were interested noises. The truth was, she was strangely mesmer-ized. Maybe Sadie had slipped her something in the hot chocolate. Or perhaps the surfeit of pink was freezing her brain.

'Here's the thing, Fran. I've always liked you. I've been saying to people for *years* that if you could only lose some weight and pay a bit more attention to personal grooming, you'd be quite popular.' Sadie gave a syrupy smile and a delectable giggle. 'But it's more than that. You and that Asian hottie of yours have been making waves. People are talking about it. A lot. In fact, me and Robbie are starting to feel like old news – which sorta sucks.'

Okaaay. Was this some kind of official warning? Fran found it hard to believe she could pose a threat to Sadie's reign of unstoppable social conquest, but if the lessons of history were to be believed, all dictators were paranoid neurotics underneath. Perhaps she might have been more intimidated if she wasn't going up against a psychotic time-travelling witch in a few hours' time. As it was, the whole situation was laughable.

'Look, Sadie, I'm sorry if I've got in your way or anything. But you don't have to worry, because I'm really not interested in—'

Sadie shushed her. 'You're not in my way, silly! In fact, I *admire* how far you've come. It's, like, *inspirational* . . . See, I've always somehow managed to have it all: the prom-queen looks, the cool boyfriend, the effortless popularity. But lately there's – well, there's been a certain amount of disruption to the status ho.'

'Status . . . quo?'

'Like I said. Take me and Zara, for example. My chat with you yesterday forced home how much things have changed between us. You remember – when you told me how Zara really thinks I'm a brain-dead groupie with a one-track mind.'

Hmm. This was interesting.

'Bitching about me behind my back was *so* the last straw. That's, like, the *ultimate* betrayal.'

'I can imagine.'

'See, what ordinary people don't seem to realize is that it takes a lot of effort to stay at the top. Structure and strategy. And me and Zara had it sorted.'

Fran nodded. The Gruesome Twosome operated as an alliance: good cop, bad cop. Everyone knew that. So why would Zara want to mess with it? Still, from the way Sadie was talking, it seemed that things hadn't been well for a while. And her next words confirmed it.

'But lately,' she said, 'the dynamic's broken down. Zara hasn't pulled anyone hot for *ages*. Instead, she spends all her time whining about the Good Old Days and is totally uninterested in me and Robbie and the band and *anything* cool. I reckon she's losing it – big time.' She sighed and began to fiddle with a toy unicorn. 'I can see I'm gonna have to level with you here, Fran. To be honest, the Oxymorons' credibility isn't what it – or Firedog's – was. Maybe Zara even had a point about Quinn and Robbie and their stupid feud . . . Anyway, I'm, like, totally thrilled they're gonna be buddies again. But that's only part of it. It's easy to create a buzz, right, but it's much harder to maintain it. You need new structures, new strategies. New *personalities*. You hear what I'm saying?'

Fran's head was reeling. If she'd understood right, Sadie was inviting her to be the New Zara.

Sadie obviously took her silence for breathless excitement. 'Ever since Francesca left and you got yourself a boyfriend, you've got more assertive. More fun to be around. Better looking, even. *Every-one's* noticed it. Then I was chatting to Quinn last night, after his big reunion with Robbie, and he was saying you and Ash have been having some problems. Though I kinda guessed this from the way you and Quinn were all over each other yesterday.'

'I wouldn't read too much into—'

'Playing hard to get, huh? Treat 'em mean to keep 'em keen and all that.' Sadie landed a fake punch on her arm. 'I like your style, girlfriend! Just make sure you treat the *right* person meanly, that's all. Ash is . . . kinda exotic, yeah, but once the novelty factor wears off, he'll be in danger of being plain weird instead of weirdly cool. And that's where Quinn comes in. Quinn is *so* the best bet.'

'For what?' Fran enquired through gritted teeth.

'Security! Social status! Popularity!' Sadie beamed. 'Play your cards right, hon, and you could have the whole of Conville Secondary at your feet. Our feet, that is. You, me, Quinn and Robbie. *Together*.'

Fran hardly knew where to start. For a moment she just sat there, spluttering. 'Listen, you've got the wrong idea about me. About everything. Quinn doesn't—'

'You don't have to take my word for it, you know. He's coming over in a minute, with Robbie. The four of us are gonna have a *blast*!'

Omigod, thought Fran. It's a set up. 'I need to use your bathroom,' she said, standing up abruptly.

'Freshening yourself up before the boys arrive?' Sadie replied with a knowing smirk. 'Top of the stairs on the left. And, Franny – you might want to do something about your hair while you're at it.'

Fran clenched her fists so hard, the nails dug into her palms. She'd always known Sadie was the bimbo from hell, but up till now she shared the common perception that Zara was the really dangerous one. Not any more. At least you knew where you were with Zara: sure, she was an out-and-out bitch with psychopathic tendencies, but at least she was honest about it. Fran didn't know what made her more angry: Sadie's advice to ditch her boyfriend as soon as he lost his novelty value or the assumption that she'd be so pathetically grateful to get the chance of joining Sadie's little posse that she'd give up anything and everything to get there.

In some ways, the offer was a familiar one: the plot of a hundred chick flicks, where the one-time ugly duckling is invited to join the cool kids and sells her soul for popularity before she realizes the error of her ways. And perhaps it might even have tempted her – back in the days when she was trailing in Francesca's shadow and yearning hopelessly after Quinn. Well, those days were long gone, thank God. Instead she'd reached the point where Sadie's little proposition should have been no more than good entertainment. A story to share with Ash – something they could both look down their noses and laugh at.

Except she couldn't. Because the way things were going, she wouldn't have a boyfriend or even a mate to share *anything* with. Here was Sadie, with her pathetic schemes of prom-queen glory, while Fran was battling Dark Arts and eternal curses. She had no room for laughter. No, what she felt now was hot, hard rage.

As soon as she locked the bathroom door behind her, she summoned the genie.

'You get your way. You can have your wish.'

Zara was not about to come over all gushy with gratitude. 'You've changed your tune,' she remarked, sauntering over to the bathroom mirror and helping herself to a stray tube of lipgloss. '"Strawberry Dreams" . . . ugh. Hasn't Sadie won you over with her irresistible charm then?'

'It's *my* charm that's the point in question. In fact, your best buddy's so impressed by the New Fran she's got me lined up as your replacement.'

The genie continued applying lipgloss. 'Well, she's really scraping the barrel then, isn't she? Couldn't handle the competition, I guess, so she's looking for a sidekick-cum-doormat. Good luck to her, I say. And good luck to you – you'll need it.'

'It's not as if I'm going to take her up on her offer.'

'Oh yeah, I forgot. You've got too much integrity for all that.'

'Integrity can only get you so far,' Fran said grimly. 'You want to use a wish on vengeance? Be my guest. As long as it gets me to Leila, and there's no death or dismemberment involved, you're very welcome to do your worst.'

They were interrupted by a scratching sound at the bathroom door. It was Ash, whose dignity, as well as fur, had been severely ruffled by his ejection from Sadie's bedroom. Fran opened the door to see that some of his frustration had been taken out on its paintwork. 'What on earth were you and the Barbie doll talking about?' he asked crossly. 'You were *ages*. And while we're on the subject, I'm not some spare part to be chucked about whenever it suits you. Show some respect.'

'Like the respect you were showing Sadie when she was prancing around in her underwear?'

Before Ash could reply, Sadie's voice came floating up from the front hall.

'Fran!' she called. 'Who are you talking to up there? I'm downstairs – come and say hi to Robbie!'

Feeling relieved her latest spat with Ash couldn't progress any further, Fran hurried down to the kitchen, cat and genie in hot pursuit.

The sight that awaited them there was not for the faint-hearted. Sadie and Rob were locked in an embrace, alternately cooing and grunting in a slobber of lips, tongues, writhing bodies and wandering hands. Fran, hovering at the entrance to the kitchen, didn't know where to look. She tried a loud cough. Ash followed it up with his choking-on-a-furball number. Finally, reluctantly, the lovebirds drew apart with a prolonged squelching sound.

'Hey, Fran,' leered Rob. 'Didn't see you there.'

'That's cos you've only got eyes for your Sadie-wadie-woo,' Sadie gurgled. 'You bad boy!'

'Foxy little minx!'

'Oooh!'

'Grrrr!'

Squelch . . .

'Now you see what I'm up against,' said Zara, who was hovering at Fran's shoulder, arms folded across her chest. 'This is what I have to put up with *all the friggin' time*. And, frankly, it makes me want to heave.'

'I can see why,' said Fran, who was feeling a bit queasy herself.

'See what?' asked Rob while sucking Sadie's left earlobe.

'Why you should have been neutered at birth,' Zara shot back.

'Why the two of you are so good together,' said Fran, just as quickly. 'Bet you'll be the hottest couple at *Hype!*.'

'You got the tickets safe and sound, babe?' Rob enquired, moving from licking Sadie's earlobe to nuzzling her neck.

His girlfriend temporarily extracted herself from the slurp-fest to delve in the back pocket of her jeans. 'Right here,' she said, putting them on the worktop with a flourish. 'And I'm not letting them out of my sight – these things are, like, gold dust.' She turned to Fran. 'Such a pity you and Quinn can't go so we could make it a foursome!'

'Though I'm sure there'll be other occasions,' said Rob with a suggestive wink. Fran could practically hear Ash bristling.

'Definitely,' added Sadie. 'And talking of Quinn, shouldn't he be here by now? Franny here is super-excited about seeing him. He's all we've been talking about for the last hour . . .'

At this point, Ash lost it. 'Quinn? *Again?*' the cat burst out. 'I don't flippin' believe it!'

Fran put her hand to her mouth in horror.

'Omigod, I could've sworn I just heard Ash,' Sadie squawked, whipping her head round to peer suspiciously out of the window. 'He must be, like, *stalking* you.'

But Rob was staring at the cat with a seriously freaked-out expression. 'I, uh . . . it's the weirdest thing but y'know, I thought I . . . I think I . . .'

Fran shook her head furiously at Ash. Too late. The cat leaped up to stand on the kitchen counter and fixed Rob with his unblinking golden stare.

'*You* can *think*? Well, I guess we're all in for a shock this morning,' he said clearly.

There was a split second of silent disbelief, then

Sadie began to scream, on and on in a high shrill sound. Rob joined her, demonstrating an impressive falsetto.

'Time to make my wish, wouldn't you say?' remarked the genie.

Approximately ten seconds later, Fran, Zara and Ash were staring at two twenty-centimetre dolls that could well have come from Sadie's collection upstairs. Barbie and Ken, plastic hand in plastic hand, identical cheesy grins on their small plastic faces. The girl doll had synthetic yellow hair in a high ponytail, a trace of glitter shadow around her exaggeratedly large blue eyes, with her exaggeratedly perfect figure modelling miniature jeans and a flirty powder-blue top. The boy doll was kitted out in baggy combat trousers and a slogan T-shirt, his plastic brown hair moulded into waves. In spite of the undoubted resemblance to their human counterparts, both dolls looked as if they'd come straight off a mass-production assembly line. Once translated into plastic, Rob and Sadie's bland good looks were eerily featureless.

'Oh God, what have we done?' whispered Fran, both fascinated and appalled.

'Turned them into the plastic people they really are,' retorted the genie. 'An inspired wish, even if I do say so myself.' She went to give Sadie's yellow hair an investigative tug.

Fran got there first. 'Leave her alone. We can't start molesting them!'

'Why ever not? I was *counting* on giving Sadie's

head a little shave, maybe improving Rob with a decorative felt-tip pimple or ten . . .'

'It's no use – Fran's always been a spoilsport when it comes to vengeance wishes,' Ash told her. 'It was the same when I was her genie. She'd be fired up for a spot of retribution, then get all boring and guilty afterwards.'

'I'm sorry my sense of conscience is so tedious,' Fran retorted, stung by his disloyalty, 'but while we're on the subject of guilt, what the hell were you *doing* back there, Ash? Opening your mouth and letting any old rubbish come out – in public! You nearly ruined everything! Do it again and the men in white coats could be whisking you off to a research lab. Or a travelling circus.'

'I know it was stupid.' Ash sounded abashed. 'It's just that it feels as if Quinn is always—'

'And here he comes again,' said Zara with relish. She pointed to the kitchen window, where a familiar male form was approaching the back door.

Fran had just enough time to send Zara back into the ring, push the Rob 'n' Sadie dolls behind the bread-bin and hiss *behave!* to Ash before Quinn was rapping at the back door. When he saw it was Fran who was letting him in, he flushed a dull red.

'Er, hi, Fran.'

'Hello, Quinn.'

There was a prolonged pause while Quinn tried to think of something charming or witty to say. *Anything* to say. He'd spent most of the night brooding on his mad behaviour in the cinema and afterwards, and so when Rob had suggested he come over and hang out with him, Sadie and Fran the next morning, he thought it would be a good chance to redeem himself in Fran's eyes, or at the very least prove to her – and to himself – that he wasn't turning into a lunatic or pervert or both. Now he tugged his hair and coughed nervously. 'Look, that, er, thing with your dad last night. It wasn't – I wasn't – I didn't mean –' He ground to a halt.

'Already forgotten,' said Fran quickly, moving protectively in front of the bread-bin.

She needn't have worried: for the moment, Quinn's eyes remained fixed on the floor. 'So, you and Sadie have been hanging out this morning?'

'Sort of.'

'Cool.'

'Yeah . . . and you and Rob are mates again.'

'Looks like it.'

'Cool.'

'Yeah.'

More silence. Quinn was not best pleased to see that Fran had brought her psycho kitty along for a visit. Once again it was staring at him fixedly with its creepy yellow eyes. Quinn was not a fanciful kind of guy, but everything about that cat seemed to be exuding menace. In fact, just looking at the beast sent a shiver down his spine.

'You brought your cat,' he said at last.

'Yes. He's been a bit peaky lately, so I thought it best to keep an eye on him.'

'Poor little thing,' said Quinn, attempting to look both manly and compassionate. 'What's wrong with him?'

'He's had worms.'

The cat's tail twitched, and Fran patted it on the top of its head with what seemed like slightly unnecessary force. 'But don't worry,' she added brightly, 'Mr Cuddles is much better now. And if he knows what's good for him, he'll be on his *very* best behaviour.'

Quinn had had enough of cat talk. 'So where are Rob and Sadie – still getting ready for their big TV debut?'

Fran took a deep breath. 'Yeah . . . Funny about that. See, it turns out they can't make *Hype!* after all.'

'What?'

'I know it's weird, but when I was . . . in the bathroom . . . Sadie took a phone call. And when I came down to the kitchen, they'd both gone and left me this.' She gestured to the top, where a pink heart-shaped note was attached to the two *Hype!* tickets. Zara's forgery skills had turned out to be as impressive as her wish-making.

Franny, the note said in imitation of Sadie's curly-girlie handwriting, *Something's come up and me and Robbie can't use our tickets for* Hype! *this afternoon. But we want you to go instead and have lots of fun. Hugs and kisses and see you v. soon, love S xoxoxoxoxoxox*

'That's strange,' said Quinn, frowning. 'The entire school must've heard them banging on about *Hype!* by now. Their big TV debut and all that. Still, it doesn't sound like there was any kind of emergency . . . Hey, check it out!'

He had caught sight of the Rob doll's trainer-clad

foot poking out from behind the bread-bin. He pulled the two dolls out and started to laugh. 'I don't believe it. Sadie's dressed two old Barbie and Kens to look like her and Rob.' He shook his head. 'Gotta tell you, if one of my girlfriends did that it would creep me out a little. Though I suppose it's kind of sweet.'

'Adorable,' said Fran, snatching both dolls out of Quinn's hands. 'In fact, I'd better put them back in Sadie's bedroom. We wouldn't want anything to happen to them.'

Before Quinn could reply, she raced out of the kitchen and up the stairs to Sadie's room, where she carefully laid out the dolls among the heap of satin cushions on the bed. 'Sorry, guys,' she whispered, 'but you'll be back to normal soon – promise. And it's for a good cause.'

Could the real Sadie and Rob hear her, some-where deep inside their plastic brains? Their cheesy grins remained resolutely fixed. Fran left them there among the twinkling fairy lights and toy unicorns.

When she got back to the kitchen, she found Quinn inspecting one of the tickets by the window. 'It says here that doors open at half twelve, so if we want to get front-row seats we should probably get going in the next fifteen minutes,' he told her. 'Bet the queues will be massive.'

'Hang on – *we* should get going?'

'You're not planning on going to this thing on your own are you?' he said smoothly. 'I mean, you wouldn't want the other ticket to go to waste. Two tickets, the two of us . . . It's like fate. Especially since this time I promise to be on my best behaviour. No more flipping out.'

Fran thought fast. 'Yes, but what if *I* was the person who was flipping out? What then?'

'Huh?'

'Well, you said yourself that, when you're around me, weird things keep happening. What if I get to the studio this afternoon and all sorts of craziness kicks off?'

Quinn smiled. 'You're not going to put me off that easily. I've already glimpsed your inner wild-child, you know – and it's cool. You're a woman of mystery.' He was about to say something else, but was distracted by a tearing sound. 'Speaking of, er, wild, I think your cat is having some kind of a fit –'

Ash had got hold of one of Mrs Smith's tea towels and was viciously shredding it with his claws. Violent retching sounds were interspersed with the most un-feline-like growls.

'*Bad* cat!' Fran went to rescue the tea towel, while Ash, glaring and hissing, dug his claws in for all he was worth. 'Don't be such a baby,' she said in an undertone. 'I can't stop him coming if he wants to – the tickets aren't even mine! You've got to stop being so paranoid and possessive.'

'You know,' said Quinn, looking on from a safe distance, 'that is a cat with serious issues.'

'Tell me about it.'

Quinn spent most of the trip to the TV studios attempting to prove his cat-loving credentials. He even tried to draw Fran into a discussion about sending Mr Cuddles to an animal psychologist – 'It sounds like a gimmick, but there are a lot of deeply troubled domestic pets out there. There was a whole documentary about it on Channel Five: *Pets from Hell*. Did you see it?' Ash, banished to his bag, with the zip opened the minimum amount for air, was left to fume in silence. And serve him right, thought Fran, who was still annoyed with him about . . . well, pretty much everything.

It was just as well they'd left Sadie's house in good time: when they arrived at their destination, forty-five minutes before filming was due to begin, there was already a queue outside the doors. Although the TV studios were a bit disappointing from the outside – a sprawl of dingy concrete at the edge of an industrial estate – their fellow ticket-holders made for an intimidatingly cool line-up. Fran was sure she was the youngest, as well as the least glamorous, person there, and was suddenly very glad of Quinn's company.

Of course, it would take more than small talk to distract her thoughts from what lay in wait behind the doors. But in spite of the traumas ahead, she was also curious. How would a princess straight out of the *Arabian Nights* go about hosting a twenty-first-century chat show? What Dark Arts would she use to charm the likes of Bliss Danone and a load of unwashed indie rockers?

A girl in a *Hype!* T-shirt was going down the line, handing out promotional flyers. 'Excuse me,' said Fran. 'Can you tell us anything more about Posy's replacement? The guest presenter, I mean.'

The girl's eyes glazed over. Her monotone took on an almost robotic precision. 'Leila Arrabiata, the

Babe of Baghdad, is the biggest thing to come out of the Middle East since the invention of zero. We're incredibly lucky to have her and I know she's going to be a raging success. Have a nice day!' She blinked, flashed them a smile as rigid as the Sadie doll's, and moved off.

'Babe of Baghdad, huh? Maybe Ash knows her,' Quinn grinned. 'Stranger things have happened.'

'Ha ha,' said Fran weakly. Everyone in the queue was swapping theories as to the truth behind Posy's 'exhaustion'; most of which were along the lines that Zara had suggested. But as Fran listened to the *Hype!* rep giving the exact same speech to someone behind them, she realized she should have guessed it would take more than hexing Posy to get Leila on to the show. By the sound of it, Leila had turned the whole production company into a gang of zombies . . .

The next moment the doors had opened and, before she knew it, they had handed their tickets over and were shuffling through to the security check. Quinn had been incredulous when he'd heard Fran was planning on smuggling her pet into the TV studios, yet somehow, though he couldn't for the life of him work it out, the cat got through without anybody seeming to notice. As a matter of fact, Fran had simply summoned Zara to hold the cat-carrier while Fran and her handbag were being checked. Since anything the invisible genie was holding became invisible too, Ash managed to slip past without any fuss and Zara disappeared into the ring soon afterwards.

Once past security, they came to a scruffy lounge

area, where they had to wait for another ten minutes before everyone was allowed into the studio to bag their seats. The set looked a lot smaller and flimsier than it did on TV: tiers of seating curved around the two interconnecting stages, one with tables and sofas, and the other set up with music equipment. Both stages had a backdrop of massive screens, blank except for the *Hype!* logo, and were still being checked over by the technical crew. Fran supposed she should be relieved there was no sign of *Night of the Living Dead* type activity; everyone looked focused but relaxed, professionals following a familiar routine. In fact, the only thing out of place was a gold throne-like chair, plonked among the sofa-and-table arrangement. It could be there as a homage to Bliss Danone, this week's star guest, but somehow Fran didn't think so.

Quinn, meanwhile, was surprised to find Fran heading for a seat that, although on the front row, was partly obscured by a large monitor. He was even more surprised when she reached into her bag and began putting on the oversized cap, scarf and dark glasses she'd smuggled in with the cat.

But before Quinn could ask her what was going on, the floor manager came out and everyone had to shut up while he explained various rules and regulations, and what to do in case of an emergency (Fran, at least, found herself listening to this last one with more than usual concentration). He ended his speech with all the reasons why *Hype!* was the hottest entertainment show on the box, possibly the planet – before launching into the exact same spiel about their new presenter as had the girl they'd talked to while queuing.

At the mention of Leila, there was some discontented muttering from the hard-core Posy fans in the audience. A bloke sitting behind Fran grumbled about being fed a load of PR bull – 'Nobody *I* know has ever heard of this girl. Sounds like some kind of multicultural diversity stunt.' His mate was equally suspicious: 'That Arrabiata's some kind of pasta sauce, innit?' But the mood improved with the arrival of the warm-up man, who soon got everyone laughing and cheering, and practising their applause.

'So,' said Quinn, halfway into a joke about a group of Scientologists at a baby shower, 'how's it feel to be making your second TV appearance?'

It was true that Fran had, in fact, been on TV fairly recently, as the unwitting stooge to a boy magician. She still writhed with shame whenever she thought about it.

'Don't remind me,' she groaned from behind a layer of scarf. 'All that seems a lifetime ago, thank God.'

'Yeah, I think we were both different people back then,' he said earnestly. 'I feel like I've done a lot of growing up since.'

'I'm sure you have.'

This was a good opportunity to look deeply and meaningfully into her eyes, but Quinn was hampered by the fact that in Fran's new get-up, only her nose and upper lip were visible. He settled on squeezing her hand gently instead. Unnoticed by both of them, Ash managed to stick out his paw and, by dint of much wriggling, aimed a swipe at Quinn's leg. He missed.

By the time the comic came to the end of his routine, Fran was queasy with nerves. It was already getting hot under the studio lights, and the sight of several very heavy items of equipment swaying above their heads was making her feel faint. Still, it was easier to worry about a monitor falling down and crushing her to death than to start thinking about all the holes in their plan . . . or all the thunderbolts Leila was probably keeping tucked in her handbag. Once again, she tried to estimate the distance between her seat and the gold throne, and checked, for the hundredth time since she'd left Sadie's, that she had the curse bracelet safe in her pocket. Any minute now . . .

In the event, Leila's arrival was a bit of an anticlimax. She and Zed appeared from a side door and simply wandered on to the stage, to a chorus of ragged cheers. Zed grinned and looked around vaguely, but Leila paused to receive the acclaim with a regal wave of her hand, before mincing over to the throne. That got her some laughter, and a few wolf whistles too. If the laughter displeased her, her frown was obscured by one of the make-up girls, swooping in for a last minute touch-up.

Their new host was certainly dressed for the part. She was wearing silver combat trousers, a low-cut camisole printed with skulls, and hot-pink stilettos (though it seemed the novelty of walking on heels was causing her trouble – her progress on to the stage had been a slow and somewhat unsteady one). Perched on top of her head was a jewelled tiara that

Fran was fairly sure she recognized from Oronames's shop. If she was wearing a curse charm, however, Fran couldn't see it. The Babel stone was the only ornament around her neck.

Zed looked much the same as always, although it was hard to tell if his glazed expression and slightly jerky movements were symptoms of black magic, or if he was just as wooden in real life as he was on screen. Like Naz said, Posy was the presenter people paid attention to, the one who came up with the quirky questions, the smart one-liners and the cheeky asides.

Even without their idol, however, the audience was determined to make the most of the afternoon, and – all fired up by the warm-up man – roared with enthusiasm as soon as the countdown to transmission began. Fran closed her eyes, uttered a brief prayer and crossed as many fingers as she could manage as the applause reached a crescendo and the cameras started to roll.

The next moment, Zed had launched into his customary drawl. 'Afternoon, dudes . . . Or, for all you student dope-fiends out there – good morning!'

There were knowing sniggers from the crowd.

He tried to keep up the banter, but without Posy chipping in it all fell rather flat. 'OK, people, enough of the wisecracks,' he said with a half-hearted grin. 'The good news is, we've got a whole heap of treats for you this afternoon, and top of the list—'

'Is me, of course,' Leila cut in with a dazzling smile. 'Your hostess with the mostest, the Damsel of Deliciousness and Babe of Baghdad.'

She got a few more wolf whistles. But there was some muttering too.

Zed, shifting about uncomfortably, cleared his throat. 'Yeah . . . totally . . . right on . . . A big hand, please, for our first guest – singer, activist, style icon and all-round superstar Bliss Danone!'

A fanfare of trumpets rang out, and the sliding doors behind the main stage drew open with a puff of glitter and dry ice, as Bliss sashayed on to the set. Leila looked put out: even though *Hype!* did this sort of thing on a strictly tongue-in-cheek basis, she obviously thought it was the kind of entrance she should have made. She sat a little straighter in her throne.

In any other circumstances, Fran would have been riveted by the sight of Bliss Danone sitting only a couple of metres away. Like her or loathe her, the woman was a legend. She'd started off doing backing vocals in the seventies before finding fame in the punk explosion of the eighties and a romance with rock 'n' roll hellraiser Rich Withers. More recently, Bliss had reinvented herself as a jazz singer and animal-rights activist. Her eerily ageless face regularly featured in glossy magazines, usually accompanied by a baby seal or an orphaned bear cub.

'Howdy, folks,' she purred, crossing long black-leather-clad legs and flicking back her mane of red hair.

It seemed Zed was taking charge of the interview. At any rate, he launched into a rambling intro about how thrilled everyone was that Bliss was in the UK to pick up her Lifetime Achievement Award at next week's Quicksilvers – and how proud she must be of her four decades in the music industry.

Leila had been looking bored, but now she perked up. 'Four decades? Really? How remarkable!' she exclaimed, leaning forward in genuine interest. 'You look barely a day past twenty.'

Bliss looked gracious. 'So people keep saying. And I tell everyone the same thing: green tea. That's my beauty secret. Green tea and a tranquil mind.'

'Green tea?' Leila laughed heartily. 'What nonsense! Why, it's plain that you have drunk from the Elixir of Eternal Youth.'

The audience tittered, aware that this was something new. *Hype!* liked to be edgy, but at the end of the day it was fundamentally respectful of the almighty power of celebrity.

Bliss was both confused and belligerent. '*Liquor* has nothing to do with it. I haven't touched a drop of alcohol since my stint in rehab ten years ago,' she said icily. 'As you would know, if you'd read the third volume of my bestselling biography, *Fits and Starts*.'

'I'm sorry if you find the subject uncomfortable,' Leila said sweetly. 'I don't wish to be rude. I was brought up to be respectful towards the elderly. And, you know, I don't look my age either – technically speaking, my birth predates yours by several centuries . . . Would you like to know *my* beauty secret?'

Bliss's eyes bulged.

'Daily baths in ass's milk. Perhaps you should try it.'

'*Ass* milk?' Bliss demanded, her nasal American

whine going up several octaves. 'What the hell is that supposed to mean?'

By this point, the audience was rocking with laughter. Fran looked around at them in disbelief. She could hardly believe it, but somehow, against all the odds, Leila was turning out to be a hit.

'It's supposed to work wonders on ageing skin. Of course, some swear by washing in the blood of virgins, but each to her own,' Leila said blithely, before deciding it was time to (more or less) return to the script. 'Now, apparently you're some kind of showgirl. Perhaps you could tell us about your routine.'

'My career has been a triumph of—'

'Can you do the Scheherazade Split?'

'The what?'

'It's what all the high-class dancing girls are doing these days. Or so I'm told. Of course, being of noble birth, I wouldn't dream of performing in public myself. That's generally for slaves and concubines . . . Tell me, what makes you different from the all rest?'

'I refuse to answer such an offensive question.' Bliss's inflated lips were pursed so tightly it was a wonder the collagen wasn't spurting out. Meanwhile, poor Zed had the air of a rabbit trapped in the headlights. He kept tapping his earpiece, presumably in the hope of rescue or intervention. None came.

'Dear me, you must have *some* kind of distinguishing feature! Can you charm snakes? Make grapes pop out of your belly button? I'm sure one of those cute performing monkeys would do wonders for your act . . . No? What a shame.' Leila shook her head regretfully, then turned to the nearest camera. 'And on the subject of dumb animals,' she said brightly, 'stay with us until after the break, when the Polar Chimps will be showcasing their latest hit. We'll be back in five!'

Right on cue, transmission was cut. A buzz of comment and exclamation immediately filled the studio. By the sounds of it, everyone had decided Leila was some kind of subversive comic genius. 'Wow, I can't believe they let her get away with all that stuff,' Quinn said to Fran. He glanced admiringly at the princess. 'And she's a total babe too.'

On stage, Bliss had got to her feet. 'I have never been so insulted in all my life,' she hissed, patches of red high on her cheeks. 'Your treatment of me has been vile and degrading and I won't stand for it.' She swept off towards the stage door and into the arms of her entourage. Zed put his head in his hands.

Fran decided her time had come. The monitors said she had 140 seconds until they were back on air and the Polar Chimps were already taking their places in the performance area. She touched Ash lightly on the head, and then released Zara from the ring. For a moment, the two girls' eyes met. Zara gave a brisk nod, then she marched on to the stage and up to the throne.

All that anybody else saw was Leila's neck jerk forward, accompanied by a choking sound. The next second she let out a screech, grabbed at the air and began looking around wildly.

* * * * * 165 * * * * *

It was too late of course – Zara had already passed on her prize and returned to the ring. Fran put her cap, scarf and dark glasses to one side, stood up from her seat and waved. 'Hello, Leila,' she said clearly, 'it's Fran. We have to talk.'

Leila was clutching her neck. Everyone else – from the lead singer of the Chimps to the make-up lady with the powder puff – was looking from one girl to the other, confused, but not yet alarmed. Quinn, shrinking back into his seat, was slack-jawed in disbelief. Since when did Fran speak fluent Arabic?

'As you've probably realized, I've got your Babel stone translator,' Fran continued as calmly as she could. 'And I'm not going to give it back until you come outside and speak to me.'

'How *dare* you!' Leila spluttered. 'You won't get away with this!'

Fran risked a glance at the nearest security guards. They might not be able to understand any of this exchange, but they knew trouble when they saw it and were already poised for action. The floor manager was muttering into his walkie-talkie. The cameramen and technicians were exchanging looks. Twenty seconds until they were on air . . .

'Don't try anything,' she told Leila quickly. 'If there's any trouble, I'll use a wish to get rid of the stone and you'll be incommunicado for the next seven hours. Smile, wave, and walk off with me like it's the most natural thing in the world.' She turned to Zed and switched back to English. 'Sorry for the interruption, but Leila and I are going to have a little backstage chat. Are you OK to hold the fort for a while?'

He nodded dumbly. The security guards warily resumed their positions. The cameramen and technicians shrugged and turned back to the job in hand. The audience, still buzzing, settled back in their seats. Five seconds to go.

Fran made her way out of the side exit and into a corridor leading to the presenters' dressing rooms. No one stopped her. A few moments later, Leila came tottering after her, face ablaze. Fran found she was grateful for those hot-pink stilettos – they were probably the only thing preventing Leila from lunging at her, tooth and nail.

As it was, Leila settled for a very wobbly stamp of her foot. 'Give me back my stone! At once! You're spoiling *everything*!'

Stilettos or no, Fran knew she was living on borrowed time. She made her voice as soothing as possible, trying to think of the sort of grovelling Ash would do.

'Incredibly Awesome Princess, please accept my apologies for the disruption and, er, any inconvenience caused. All I want is—'

'I'm not a princess any more! I'm a celebrity!'

Fran decided to press on with the flattery. 'That's right – you're a celebrity! Amazing! You know, it takes most people *years* to get on TV, and here you are, an instant hit! I can't imagine how you did it!'

There was a pause. Leila was clearly torn between tearing strips off Fran and gloating over her achievements. Vanity won. At any rate, she allowed herself a superior smirk. 'Oh, it wasn't that hard. After our chat in the bar, I cast a handful of runes to locate this Posy girl. She was here, as it happens, going through arrangements for today's show.'

'So what did you do to her?'

Leila preened. 'It's commonly referred to as a coup curse – very popular with politicians and disgruntled younger sons, I believe. You use it to drain someone of their powers and then take their place.'

'OK, so you, er, drained Posy and then hypnotized everyone working with her?'

'Of course not! Hypnotism is for amateurs. No, the best thing about this particular curse, you see, is that once you've usurped the throne or whatever it is, you inherit your target's servants and entourage. It's ever so clever.'

'I see.' Fran took a deep breath. It had never been so important, or so difficult, to keep her feelings under control and her voice calm. 'But here's the thing. I'm pretty sure your ever-so-clever curse is part of the bracelet that's my only hope of setting Ash and Zara free. The bracelet of curses that you said had been given away – remember?'

Leila looked sulky. 'I only kept one back for insurance. After all, here I was, wrenched out of my own time and country, adrift in a barbarian land – a poor, lone, defenceless female—'

'But you knew from the start that I couldn't destroy the bracelet as long as you were still hanging on to a charm!'

'In all the excitement, it must have slipped my mind. I'm sorry if you went to any trouble over it.'

'Well, can – can I have it now? Please?'

'Oh dear me no, I couldn't allow that! You see,

if you were to destroy the bracelet then *all* the curses would be undone. Including the one that's set me up so nicely here.' The princess flicked an imaginary speck of dust from her skull-adorned camisole, then smiled disarmingly. 'Tell you what – how about we call it quits? You forgive my little mix-up, and I'll forget about your whole mugging-by-genie thing.' She put her hand out for the Babel stone. 'I do hope you haven't scratched it – that piece is a family heirloom, you know. It's insured for three vaults of treasure and a spice warehouse.'

'It's not a "little mix-up", it's people's lives and—'

Leila lunged, quick as lightning. The high heel of one her shoes immediately twisted under her, but as she tumbled to the ground she flung her arms round Fran's legs and brought Fran crashing down at the same time. There was a snarling sound as Ash – who'd only just managed to push his way through the swing doors – streaked past and leaped into the fray. Fran was desperately trying to hold on to the stone with one hand and activate the ring and genie with the other. Trying to get at the ring, however, proved to be a fatal distraction. With a savage thrust of her elbow, the princess sent Ash flying, then clamped her teeth down hard on Fran's right hand. Fran yelled, Ash yowled and Leila let out a whoop of triumph. The next moment, she was in a high-speed hobble back into the studio, the Babel stone clenched in her fist.

Fran dashed after her. The show had been back on air for several minutes now, the cameras trained on to the second stage, where the Chimps were droning through the refrain of 'Freakshow Requiem'.

Even so, Fran didn't pause. Everyone would think she was a deranged fan, or some nutter desperate for her fifteen seconds of televisual fame. She'd probably be prosecuted for assault and public disorder. They'd show her craziness on those endless 'Fifty Wildest TV Moments' shows. But at this point, frankly, she had nothing to lose. Blind rage, the kind that had swept over Sabrina at the wedding, surged through her.

'You witch!' she yelled, thundering towards where Leila, battered but triumphant, was climbing back on to her throne. 'You think you can treat people like dirt and get away with it! Well, you're wrong—'

'Guards,' said Leila icily, and in English once more, 'arrest this madwoman. And get that animal out of here.'

And the next minute, two very burly security guards had seized Fran by the arm. Meanwhile, the floor manager swept up Ash in an immense padded jacket and carried him out of the studio, his cries of protest muffled by three layers of polyester wadding.

Time slowed. Fran was dimly aware of the audience's gasps of excitement and alarm, of Zed and the Chimps, frozen in disbelief, of the frantic scurrying of the technical crew as transmission was cut. Well, that's one good thing, she thought blearily as the heavies began to drag her towards the doors. Then, through the bleariness, she became aware that someone was shouting her name.

It was Quinn, who for some reason had got up to stand on his seat. 'If you're going to eject her,' he announced in ringing tones, 'then you'll have to eject me first.'

Two more security guards looked at each other, shrugged and lumbered over. Quinn didn't try to resist, but kept his head high and his expression martyred.

'Stop.' Leila held up a hand to halt the eviction process. She was staring at Quinn with fascination. 'And who, pray, are you?'

'Quinn Adams, your, er, honour. I'm a friend of Fran's. But I'm primarily a musician and a song-writer.' He tried to turn and smile into the nearest camera, a futile gesture, since a) his escort immediately jerked him in the opposite direction and b) transmission had already been cut. 'I have my own band, called Firedog, and it's—'

'Yes, yes,' said Leila impatiently. 'Guards, bring the two prisoners on stage.'

The guards obliged. By now, Zed was in a cata-tonic state, rocking from side to side and moaning gently. The Chimps, like the audience, were slack-jawed and open-mouthed.

'So,' Leila said, settling back on the throne and surveying her two captives with interest. 'You two know each other.'

'More than that. I – I love her,' proclaimed Quinn, garnishing the Prince Valiant performance with chocolate-syrup tones and puppy-dog eyes. As one, the female portion of the audience let out a tender sigh.

Leila pouted. 'Fran, you naughty girl! All this hullabaloo about Ashazrahim when all the time you've got a back-up princeling to play with! How do you explain this?'

The bite-mark on Fran's right hand was going an unpleasant purple and yellow colour. The hot lights on the stage were making her dizzy, the white faces of the audience were a blurring, heaving sea. 'I want Ash,' she mumbled. 'Why can't you people just *see* that?'

'He's not good enough for you,' Quinn said virtuously.

'Quite right,' Leila agreed. 'It seems we both have Fran's best interests at heart. I just wish she could appreciate that being a celebrity is in *my* best interests too. Then we could all live happily ever after.' She smiled into the nearest camera, apparently unaware that filming had stopped.

The audience rustled. Now that all the shouting in Arabic had ended and they didn't appear to be at the centre of a terrorist plot, the situation had become rather intriguing. Most people were beginning to think it was some kind of publicity stunt.

Fran, too, had begun to recover. 'But you don't want to be a celebrity,' she said earnestly. 'Celebrities have horrible addictions and nervous breakdowns and awful relationships. Plus, most are only famous for a couple of years or so, and then everyone forgets about them unless they eat worms in the jungle or learn how to foxtrot on reality TV.'

'A couple of years? But I've been doing this for barely fifteen minutes!'

At this, the lead Chimp cleared his throat. 'Actually,' he said, 'the girl's got a point. Being famous isn't half as much fun as it's cracked up to be. Right, lads?'

There was a chorus of agreement from his fellow Chimps. 'As soon as you achieve any kind of success, the critics get their knives out,' said one. 'People say they love you, then sell your most intimate secrets to the press,' said another. 'The endless round of parties and awards ceremonies?' said the third. '*Totally* soul-destroying.'

'Though,' said the lead singer thoughtfully, 'you do get cool goodie bags.'

'Please, Leila,' Fran tried again. 'You don't want to be a celebrity and I *really* want Ash.'

'Who's Ash?' shouted out a daring member of the audience.

'My boyfriend and her ex!' Fran called back. 'Leila's, er . . . not letting us see each other! Gate-crashing the show was my only hope of getting her to change her mind.' She decided not to complicate things by bringing curses and genies into the equation.

'So who's the blond who says he's in love with you?' asked the lead Chimp, scratching his head.

'Hi there, I'm Quinn and I'm a singer-songwriter. I'm in a band called Firedog and I'd just like to say I'm a huge fan of your work. In fact—'

'Why won't she let you see this Ash bloke then?' interrupted one of Fran's security guards. He had relinquished his grip on his captive, but was cracking his knuckles in a menacing sort of way.

'It's for her own good!' Leila pouted. 'Honestly, he's the most awful boy. Ashazrahim has always been insufferably sarcastic and argumentative, vain as a peacock, contrary as a camel and stubborn as mule.'

'Well, yeah . . .' 'Fran admitted. 'But—'

'There you go!' said the princess triumphantly. 'If you can't even prove to me he's your heart's desire I don't see why I should go to the trouble of giving up mine.'

At this, Fran felt a faint, very faint, flutter of hope. 'What if I could prove that he is though? And showed you that this kind of life isn't what you truly want?'

'Hah! I'll believe it when I see it.'

'Then you will,' said Fran as she reached for the ring.

Meanwhile, the audience – who knew a cue when they heard one – broke into cheers. This was much more fun than listening to a bunch of whiny indie rockers. 'Let's see what you got, girl!' 'Show us the love, baby!'

'God in heaven!' said Zara a second or two later. 'I can't believe you've turned our rescue operation into the *Jerry Springer Show*.'

'It's a long story,' Fran muttered out of the side of her mouth. 'Bear with me, OK? This might be our last chance.' She turned to face the audience again. 'And now, ladies and gentlemen, I want you to see what me and Leila really, *really* want. In fact, I wish for our hearts' desires to be revealed.'

And, suddenly, the *Hype!* logo disappeared from screens that formed the backdrop to the stage. Instead, the view shown there and on the monitors throughout the studio was that of the Roper-family kitchen, unfeasibly immaculate, and bathed in golden light. In the midst of this soft-focus haze, Fran and Ash were sitting at the table, holding hands and smiling into each other's eyes. Perhaps Fran was a little thinner and Ash was dressed a little more conservatively than usual. Behind them, the rest of the Roper family looked on with doting expressions. 'Son,' Mr Roper was saying, 'it was a truly blessed day when you came into Fran's life.' Violin music soared romantically in the background.

Fran let out a deep, wavering breath. Thank God. 'That's all I want,' she said simply. 'Do you see?'

The audience whooped their approval. Even Quinn found himself joining the applause.

Leila sniffed. But the display wasn't over. Quickly, the images on the screens changed to the interior of an ornate marble palace. Leila was seated on an immense throne, next to a small, nervous-looking little man in a turban. She was dressed in shimmering silks and dripping in jewels, a vast crown on her head, while a procession of people prostrated themselves before her. 'My goodness! That's the sultan!' the princess exclaimed.

'See,' said Fran, 'you don't really want to be a twenty-first-century celeb. You want to be a queen – a proper queen – back in times when that actually meant something. Homage and riches and adoring slaves! Think of all the fun you could have!'

Leila frowned. 'Yes . . . maybe. But . . . but why can't I have homage and riches and adoring slaves *here*?' She gestured towards the stands.

This was a mistake: although the production team and camera crew, who were still under the influence of the coup curse, began to applaud ingratiatingly, the studio audience was less receptive. In fact, the majority were shaking their heads and muttering in a disgruntled manner. There was even a catcall from the back.

'It won't last,' said Fran sagely. 'They're already beginning to turn on you, I'm afraid. And the thing with the public these days,' she added, 'is that you can't execute them when you stop being popular.'

'Really? Are you *sure*? In that case . . . well, perhaps you're right. I *have* always fancied being queen of all I surveyed. And I admit it would be a relief to return to civilized footwear.' The princess eyed her stilettos with distaste, sighed, and felt within the zip pocket of her combat trousers. 'Oh all right. Here you go.'

With her heart in her mouth, Fran received the final and last charm, which was in the shape of a spiky crown. Her hands were shaking so much it took a few minutes for her to fix it to the tiny wire loop on the bracelet. Ignoring the confused background grumbling, Fran laid the curse bracelet on the floor. 'But wait – where's A – where's my cat?' she asked, seized by a new fear. In all the drama she'd lost track of his whereabouts.

'They chucked him out by the rubbish bins,' the genie informed her. 'Best place for him.'

Fran was inclined to agree. At least this way his transformation would be out of the public eye. And, all things considered, she was relieved he'd missed her widescreen proclamation of eternal lurve. His ego was quite big enough already. With clammy hands and a thundering heart, she stamped her left heel down on the bracelet: once, twice, three times.

Please, God . . . please . . .

Nothing happened. In fact, the metal was barely dented.

'I'd stay well back if I were you,' the princess remarked. 'Black magic always—'

But her words were lost in a roll of thunder. This was followed by an extremely loud bang, a flash, and an immense cloud of dark smoke whose sulphurous fumes set everyone in the studio choking and spluttering. Several people started screaming. The emergency lights came on. So did the sprinkler system. A stampede for the exits followed, while various studio officials attempted to wave their arms and shout instructions in a soothing manner.

The entire stage was still engulfed in smoke. Fran's eyes burned, her whole body was racked by coughs. She lurched round blindly, arms flailing, and managed to smack somebody in the face. There was a grunt and a curse. Something about that curse was familiar . . . And now someone was grasping her by the shoulders and saying her name. Someone with black hair and bronze skin and eyes every bit as red and streaming as hers. '*Ash!*' she yelled hoarsely. '*Ash!*' And found she was laughing and crying and coughing all at once.

And so it was that the handful of people still staggering about in the studio as the smoke began to disperse, witnessed the heart-warming spectacle of Fran entangled with a tall foreign-looking boy with a black eye, a girl with spiky boots and even spikier hair wrapped around the Prince Valiant blond, while Leila – not to be outdone – was snogging the face off the nearest available Chimp. Briefly, the screens and monitors cleared of static to display fireworks and multicoloured stars. The surviving spectators broke into applause. And everyone on the stage drew apart briefly and blinked, before joining hands for a slightly wobbly bow. It seemed the appropriate thing to do.

Leila stepped forward with a radiant smile. 'Thank you ever so much for having me. I've had a simply *marvellous* time.' In the distance, the wail of approaching sirens could be heard. 'But now I'm afraid I really must be off.' She produced a small square of material from her pocket and snapped her fingers commandingly. A moment later, she was standing in the centre of a full-sized carpet. 'Good luck, Fran, you funny girl! I *do* hope you don't end up getting your heart broken. Ash – when all's said and done, I suppose I forgive you. And, Zara – perhaps next time you'll remember that discretion is the better part of valour.'

'Yeah, and perhaps next time the sultan'll stick a scimitar up your—'

Fran clapped her hand over Zara's mouth before she could go any further. And in the blink of an eye and a shimmer of purple haze, both princess and carpet were gone.

Even without a magic carpet, the second getaway of the afternoon went remarkably smoothly as, under cover of the general chaos, Ash led Fran, Zara and Quinn through the backstage route he'd used on his return (in cat form) from the rubbish bins. In the rainy car park outside, an emergency evacuation of the entire studio complex was in progress. The four of them were able to slip away down a side street before any awkward questions could be asked. Everyone looked rather shell-shocked. Quinn, in fact, had lost the power of speech and was merely gibbering. 'Wait here,' Fran instructed the others, 'and I'll go find us some taxis.'

She limped wearily towards a minicab office. Before she got there, however, a limousine with tinted windows pulled up alongside. One of the windows rolled down to reveal an improbably smooth face and an improbably red mane of hair. It was Bliss Danone.

'You,' she said. 'I'd know you anywhere! You're the crazy chick who tried to attack the *Hype!* presenter. The one who just got the show taken off air!'

Fran gulped. Inside the limo, she saw a flat-screen TV had been set into the back of one of the seats. The *Hype!* channel was currently showing repeats of old music videos.

'Now,' Bliss continued, 'as a pacifist, I never condone violent protest. However, what you did back there . . . let's just say that I appreciated your loyalty. I've always liked to think I attract a truly devoted following.'

Devoted following? Well, if Bliss thought Fran's intervention had been on her behalf, there was no point in disillusioning her. 'Leila was out of control. It made me angry, that's all. I mean, *somebody* had to take a stand.'

Bliss smiled graciously. 'Quite right. I hope you won't be in any legal bother as a result?'

Fran tried to imagine the powers that be at *Hype!* coming out of their zombification and contemplating a wrecked studio set, a hysterical audience, an AWOL presenter and an hour of so of wholly incomprehensible chaos. 'To be honest, I think they'll have other priorities.'

'Well, that's a relief,' said Bliss, applying lipstick with a lavish hand. 'Your gesture touched me deeply, it really did, and never let it be said that I don't appreciate the loyalty of my fans. If there's anything I can do—'

At this point, inspiration struck.

'Actually,' Fran cut in, 'there is . . . How about five VIP tickets to next week's Quicksilver Awards?'

Bliss blinked. There was a long, measuring sort of pause. 'Get in touch with my press officer,' she said at last, reaching out to hand Fran a business card. 'I'll instruct her to sort something out. But if you pull another stunt like today I'm afraid I'll have to take out a restraining order.'

Then she rolled up the window and the limo pulled away.

They said goodbye to Zara and Quinn at the mini-cab office. Quinn had recovered the power of speech, though he was still gibbering. 'But I just don't *get* it,' he kept on saying plaintively. 'I don't get *anything*.'

'Believe me, babe, it's better that way,' Zara retorted, slinging her arm around his shoulders. Quinn looked, if anything, even more nervous.

'So, I guess I'll see you guys at, er, school tomorrow—' Fran started.

'Not if I see you first,' sniffed Zara. She paused. 'I still don't like you, you know.'

'No.'

'And don't expect me to be grateful. It was your fault all this rubbish happened in the first place.'

'Um . . .'

'And you'd better not bring up any of this whacked-out craziness ever again. As far as I'm concerned, it never happened.'

'OK.'

'But,' she said, glaring, '*but*, all things considered . . . I'm prepared to admit you didn't screw up everything quite as much as I expected.' She paused. 'And since you and Cat Boy are the biggest freaks I've ever met, I guess that means you deserve each other. Come on, you.' And she pulled the still-gibbering Quinn into their cab.

'I can never decide who scares me the most,' Ash remarked as they settled into the back seat of their own taxi. 'Her or Leila.'

'Hmm. Personally, I found Sabrina fairly chilling. And Sadie's got hidden depths of dementedness.'

'There sure are a lot of crazy chicks out there,' he agreed, pulling her close. 'Listen, Fran I sneaked back into the studio just in time for your telly show.'

'Oh . . .' Fran found herself blushing.

'I've been a bit of a cad, haven't I?'

'Er, I think you'll find you've been a bit of a *cat*.'

'Seriously. I'm ashamed of myself. The last couple of days were hardest on you – keeping everyone going, sorting everything out – and I didn't make things any easier by getting so . . . het up . . .

about Quinn.' He bit his lip. 'This is the second time you've saved me and, frankly, I'm not sure I deserve to be your heart's desire any m—'

'Ash?'

'Yes?'

'Shut up,' said Fran very tenderly.

Aftermath

At about seven o'clock on Sunday evening, Mrs Smith came home to find Sadie and Rob in the middle of hosting a Barbie-doll's tea-party. Neither of them could explain what exactly they thought they were doing. Nor could they account for how they'd spent the rest of their day.

Still, at least they hadn't missed much at the *Hype!* recording – the scene of a publicity stunt that had disastrously backfired. The production company refused to comment on a debacle nobody, least of all themselves, understood. Instead, they devoted their energies to promoting Posy Parkin's triumphant return the following week.

Of course, rumours continued to run. The population of Conville Secondary spent a good ten minutes or so speculating about the unidentified protester glimpsed just before transmission was cut. Fran, of course, kept shtum. So did Zara and Quinn. Quinn had decided to attribute his weekend of madness to 'celebrity exhaustion' – delayed shock at the demise of his musical career and the shaving of his hair. Putting the whole horrible business firmly behind him, he threw himself into managing his and Rob's new band, the Oxydogs, and his explosive new romance with Zara Truman. Sadie's Status Ho was back with a vengeance.

Fran's reconciliation with Amira and the Butterflies coincided with the arrival of five VIP tickets to the Quicksilver Awards. According to Fran, Quinn had originally bought the tickets for Firedog, but during his self-imposed musical and social exile, didn't know what to do with them. He said Fran could have them – but only if she'd agree to go on a date with him. 'It was one of the hardest things I've ever done,' she told the others penitently, 'and in hindsight, I should have handled a lot of stuff differently. But I'd convinced myself that it'd be worth it in the end.'

Amira agreed. She was in no doubt that going to the Quicksilvers was the prelude to her conquest of the global music industry. The rest of the Butterflies weren't quite so confident of their chances of schmoozing with record producers or getting spotted by talent scouts, but their manager's optimism – and ambition – knew no bounds.

Mr and Mrs Roper continued to look on Ash with bewilderment. However, they were very impressed by a tour of the art gallery he was managing while his business partner was abroad. Ash was confident Oronames would be back before too long – 'He's a very resourceful guy' – but, just in case, was taking a part-time course in Event Management.

For Fran's birthday he gave her a charm bracelet. It didn't have any skulls or demons, but hanging next to the heart trinket was a small silver cat.

A selected list of titles available from Macmillan Children's Books

The prices shown below are correct at the time of going to press. However, Macmillan Publishers reserves the right to show new retail prices on covers, which may differ from those previously advertised.

Rose Wilkins

So Super Starry	978-0-330-42087-9	£5.99
So Super Stylish	978-0-330-43135-4	£5.99
I Love Genie: Wishful Thinking	978-0-330-43880-3	£5.99

Jaclyn Moriarty

Feeling Sorry for Celia	978-0-330-39725-7	£5.99
Finding Cassie Crazy	978-0-330-41803-0	£5.99
Becoming Bindy Mackenzie	978-0-330-43885-9	£5.99

All Pan Macmillan titles can be ordered from our website, www.panmacmillan.com, or from your local bookshop and are also available by post from:

Bookpost, PO Box 29, Douglas, Isle of Man IM99 1BQ
Credit cards accepted. For details:
Telephone: 01624 677237
Fax: 01624 670923
Email: bookshop@enterprise.net
www.bookpost.co.uk

Free postage and packing in the United Kingdom